W9-AQC-612

COLD HANDS, WARM HEART

JILL WOLFSON

COLD HANDS, WARM HEART

Henry Holt and Company
New York

Henry Holt and Company, LLC
Publishers since 1866
175 Fifth Avenue
New York, New York 10010
www.HenryHoltKids.com

Library of Congress Cataloging-in-Publication Data
Wolfson, Jill.
Cold hands, warm heart / Jill Wolfson.—1st ed.
p.   cm.
Summary: After sixteen-year-old Tyler convinces his parents to donate
the organs of his fourteen-year-old sister, who died during a gymnastics
meet, he writes letters to the recipients, including Dani, who finally has a
chance at normalcy after living fifteen years with a congenital heart defect.
ISBN-13: 978-0-8050-8282-1 / ISBN-10: 0-8050-8282-4
[1. Transplantation of organs, tissue, etc.—Fiction.   2. Medical care—
Fiction.   3. Hospitals—Fiction.   4. Interpersonal relations—Fiction.
5. Brothers and sisters—Fiction.   6. Death—Fiction.   7. Jews—United
States—Fiction.]   I. Title.
PZ7.W8332Col 2009   [Fic]—dc22   2008040594

First Edition—2009
Printed in the United States of America on acid-free paper. ∞

10   9   8   7   6   5   4   3   2   1

In memory of my bighearted dad,
Gilbert Wolfson

ACKNOWLEDGMENTS

I want to thank the many organ recipients and donor families who shared with me their personal tales. Thanks especially to Sarah Sabia, Laura Simons, and the entire Castellanos family. This was not an easy topic for them, yet they were willing to share with me the emotional complexity of the transplant experience.

Mary Burge, the social worker in the pediatric heart transplant unit at Lucile Parkard Children's Hospital, was an amazing guide. She graciously shared with me her decades of experience and insights, and introduced me to children, families, and medical staff. She encouraged me forward and read every word of this book, offering invaluable direction. Also thanks to others at LPCH who shared their stories, advice, and medical knowledge, especially Dr. David Rosenthal. Any mistakes are my own.

Cathy Olmo and Anjie Nix of the California Transplant Network provided technical details of the transplant process, their personal experiences, and perspective from the donor family's point of view. Again, any errors are my own.

A big thanks to my friend, journalist Sara Solovitch. When I told her I was thinking about writing a novel about organ donation, she immediately shared her own interviews, stories, and contacts from years of health reporting. Doors opened because of her.

Kate Farrell, my editor at Holt, encouraged this book from the beginning. Her support and editing were priceless. Ana Deboo's copyediting made this story clearer and accurate. My dear friend Nancy Redwine offered astute literary advice, cheerleading, and long beach walks. She's my cherished teacher on the subject of illness and living life fully in the midst of it. My writing group—Lisa, Karen, and Micah—volunteered at our very first meeting to tackle a draft of a couple hundred pages. They offered great advice. My nieces and nephew, Cara, Brianna, and Sean, lent me their names for characters. For the record: I do have a sister Wendy, and when she was a child, she had curly blond hair, but she was never, ever, ever a brat. Well, hardly ever.

And of course, big hugs to Alex and Gwen, my personal windows into how kids and teenagers think, talk, laugh, and love.

COLD HANDS, WARM HEART

ONE

AMANDA STOOD BEFORE THE table of judges, waiting for her turn to compete on the uneven bars. Her hair was pulled into a bun, tight enough to give anyone a headache and moussed hard and flat to her scalp. Her leotard was black velvet with a splash of sequins from the waist up, like a glamorous coat of armor cut low in the back to emphasize her muscular shoulders.

At fourteen, Amanda was short for her age, but all legs and arm strength. Her body fat measured so low that she had gotten her period only once, a thin flow of blood before it stopped and showed no sign of making another appearance. Her longtime coach, an ex-college gymnast named Dave, was secretly pleased that his star performer had cheated puberty. It kept her hips narrow, her chest as flat as a nine-year-old's. No cramps, no bloating, not the usual moaning of teenagers feeling too sick to work out. Amanda remained an arrow of a girl built for slicing through the air.

All around the gym that afternoon, a four-ring circus of flips, spins, and jumps was taking place. On the balance beam, one competitor threw a double back flip and stumbled the landing, a big deduction of points. Another girl vaulted off the pommel horse, landing with a crisp arch of her back. In a floor routine, a girl in a bright red leotard performed three lightning-speed front handsprings in a row.

As always when awaiting her turn to compete, Amanda didn't fidget. Her arms hung at her sides, like the palms were stitched to the thighs. By the lack of emotion on her face, she could have been waiting, bored, in a grocery store line. Other competitors couldn't help but let on how nervous they were, their hands clammy and their faces turning either too red or too white from the strain of reining in their emotions. There was one girl on Amanda's team who threw up before many competitions. Especially at an important one like this, the official state meet, the chance to compete in the Nationals riding on the outcome.

At this late point in the day, most of the observers—mothers and fathers, aunts, uncles, and grandparents—had sore bottoms and shifted uncomfortably in the hard bleacher seats. The little brothers and sisters of the gymnasts, bored to tears by now, swatted each other with scorecards. Everyone was breathing in the sharp, greasy smell of the nachos sold by the Booster Club.

Amanda's mother, Claire—brown-haired and green-eyed, her daughter definitely shared her coloring—sat four rows up on the stands, nervously biting her lower lip. Even though she was a gym-meet veteran of many years, her body still couldn't bear the lull leading up to when Amanda's hands first touched the bars. With a heavy sigh, Claire checked her watch. Seated next to her, another gym mom flashed a smile of empathy.

Almost directly behind Claire sat her ex-husband Robert, Amanda's father. Usually these two made a point of sitting on opposite ends of the gym, so it was an uncomfortable coincidence that they found themselves so close together. Amanda knew, of course, that both her parents were there in the bleachers, but she didn't wave, make eye contact, or acknowledge them in any way. She didn't want that kind of distraction. Just the thought of her parents being in the same room was enough to give her a stomachache. She hated the low-level tension when they were forced to be together, how they nodded at each other with pursed lips. It had been especially awful before her dad broke up with his girlfriend.

She dashed this image from her mind and brought herself back to the competition, wondering, *Why are the judges taking so long? How long could it take to add up the previous score?*

Some girls from another team (blue leotards with red and white stripes down the sides) finished their turns on the balance beam and drifted closer to the bars. They stood off to the side, waiting to get a better look at Amanda, the gymnast who was known for never flubbing a routine on the uneven bars, who never gave anyone else a chance to go home with a first-place medal. The girls stood shoulder to shoulder, sipping from water bottles and gossiping about Amanda's leotard ("too showy"), her personality ("too Little Miss Perfect"). One of the girls whispered what the others were all thinking: "Can't she miss, like, just once?"

And then, finally.

The head judge put down her pen and raised her right arm, the signal to begin. Amanda straightened her already squared shoulders and returned the salute. She flashed the kind of smile where all her teeth showed. Then her mouth collapsed into a tight, determined line. She breathed in slowly and deeply, letting the air turn her belly as hard and round as an inverted wooden bowl. With the full muscle of both legs, Amanda ran, and then hit the springboard that carried her straight up, her hands gripping the highest of the two metal bars.

That was the point where her mind shut off and

allowed her body—the muscles, tendons, bones, lungs, heart—to remember what they were trained to do.

Amanda swung forward. For a brief, breathtaking moment, she let go of the bar and hung suspended in midair before dropping and twisting just in time to grasp the lower bar. In the next swift, effortless move, she jumped back to the high bar, her body already pumping forward. The next skill required enormous strength and split-second timing. Up she went into a handstand, as if an invisible thread had pulled her into position and held her there, defying gravity.

Coach Dave clenched his fist, pumped it in the air. "Yesssss," he said with five sharp *S*'s.

The girls in blue leotards with red and white stripes rolled their eyes at each other.

Next came the giants, the straight-arm swings around the bar. Amanda loved this move best of all. Hurling her body up and over, around and around, she was always on the verge of out of control, pushing up to the danger line, right up to it. It had to be that way. That was where the top scores waited, right at the upper limit of speed and power, right up to the very treacherous edge, where other girls got scared and backed off.

There, up to *that* point, right there, nothing less.

And then.

Afterward, after it was all over, one of Amanda's

teammates swore that this was when she heard a gasp. "Like someone seeing a ghost," she said.

But the head judge, who was well trained to pick up on anything out of the ordinary—a toe not pointed, a back with a few degrees too much arch—testified she had noticed only the very slightest overrotation. "It was a beautiful routine. Until she . . . the girl . . . Amanda . . . until she just lost it."

Afterward came all the theories, theory after theory that led nowhere definitive. Her mind must have wandered. *Amanda's mind never wandered!* Maybe she had gotten scared. *Scared? Amanda, scared?* Or maybe fate was involved, one of those cruel twists. Maybe something inside her body had been programmed from birth to give out on this particular Sunday at this particular minute.

Things like that happen. In this world, such strange, strange things *do* happen.

Her body hurled forward, then dropped. No one could agree on what hit where first, only that there was a clink of bone hitting metal, then a sickening thud when Amanda landed facedown on the floor. The head judge jumped from her chair, hand pressed over her mouth. People in the stands stopped chewing their nachos.

As one unit, the girls in red, white, and blue looked down at their feet. They didn't say anything. Saying it aloud would give their collective thoughts too much weight, too much reality. Was it possible? Could *they* have caused it? When they had wished she would miss just once? Had their jealousy tapped into an evil that powerful, a force that destructive? One of the girls, struggling with a mix of guilt and horror, prayed to the air, "Get up. Get *up*."

But Amanda lay there, looking like she was asleep except for the odd, unnatural angle of her neck. Light from the overhead fluorescents played on the sequins of her uniform. A man, the father of another competitor, rushed from his seat, shouting, "I'm a doctor. Don't move her!"

In the stands, five rows back, a man grasped the shoulder of the brown-haired, green-eyed woman in front of him. Her mouth opened, but no sound came out. Claire's right arm reached across her chest and covered her ex-husband's shaking hand with her own.

TWO

WHEN DR. DAVID SILVERMAN entered room 132, he noticed that the Schecters were in much the same positions as they had been for the past two days. Robert, the father, stood with his hands resting on the ledge of the windowsill, only vaguely aware of time, unconsciously marking its passage by cars coming and going in the hospital parking lot.

Next to him, slumped in a chair, the girl's older brother, his dark hair disheveled, his legs stretched out before him, was plugged into an iPod and bent over a video game. Tuned in and tuned out. There were circles under his eyes so dark it looked like some kindergartner had painted them there. Dr. Silverman tried to recall the boy's name. Travis? Taylor? It was one of those *T* names that was so prevalent among this crop of teenage boys. Tyler. That was it.

Then there was the mother, seated next to her daughter and hovering like mothers do. Any closer and Claire's chair would have been on the bed. Amanda lay elevated on a pillow, a gray hospital blanket tucked around her, her head in a white turban towel as if she had just stepped out of the shower.

Even with IV lines snaking into her arms, Amanda looked perfect. *Achingly perfect*, her mother thought. Only the slight bruise on her cheek from when she fell. Other than that, not a scratch anywhere. Her lips pink and full. Her eyes half open, the whites clear. Her skin soft and rosy, not even one of those rare zits that would send her huffing into the bathroom.

The nurses had arranged Amanda's arms over the outside of the blanket, so that Claire could stroke the light, downy hair. Despite the antiseptic surroundings, Amanda even smelled exactly like herself. One sniff of her daughter's neck or hair would always give Claire a sense of well-being, a feeling that all was basically right in the world.

Perfect, she said to herself, and then more adjectives floated into her mind: tough, funny, beautiful, too hard on herself, proud, loving, smart, determined.

Alive.

Claire started at the sound of new footsteps in the room. When she looked up at Dr. Silverman, she smiled meekly and expectantly. Since the girl's accident and the emergency surgery, Dr. Silverman had come into this room many times to check her vital signs and to leave the family with the same message of hope mixed with caution. A large subdural hematoma, a blood clot. A lot of swelling. "Like a twisted ankle in the confined space of her skull," he had explained. "It's a time game. We have to wait and see."

But when the doctor entered the room this time, the father sensed something new and grave in the way he didn't meet anyone's eyes. He felt the avoidance like electricity traveling up his spine. "You know something. Something new," Robert said. It was not a question.

In response, Dr. Silverman dropped his head, chin to chest, only half a nod. "The most recent tests." He paused. "We've been measuring the blood flow to her brain." Another pause. "There is none."

"None," Robert repeated flatly.

The doctor offered synonyms, as if that would make his message more clear. "Zero. Negative. None."

Claire's eyes frantically tracked the doctor's face for something that would tell her that she was misunderstanding. How could these few syllables of negation—*zero, negative, none*—apply to her daughter? As Dr. Silverman forced himself to meet her look, he felt his professional detachment slipping. He wanted to tell this family . . . what? What *could* he say? Four years of medical school, two residencies at top teaching hospitals, and hundreds of surgeries performed had prepared him for probing around the brain, the most delicate part of a human being. But they didn't give him words for this horrible moment. Dr. Silverman's recourse was to retreat emotionally, to gather the threads of his own fears, sadness, and anger and tuck them away. He became all doctor again.

"Terrible business," he said. "I'm sorry. I've declared her brain-dead."

"No." Claire said the word simply, as if correcting one of the students in her sixth-grade class who had just given the wrong answer to a math problem.

"I'm sorry," the doctor repeated. "Truly."

One by one, the mother's features began shifting. Eyes narrowed, nostrils flared, lips sucked in on themselves. For the first time since the accident, she screamed.

All this time, Tyler had been sitting off by himself. He didn't know what he was feeling. He clicked off the iPod and removed the earphones. He watched as his mother's sister, his aunt Jen, rushed into the room from the waiting area, followed by a nurse carrying a clipboard. Soon all three women were hugging and crying. The doctor placed his hand on Robert's shoulder. Tyler heard his father groan a deep, animal sound.

Now the hospital social worker entered the room, looked around, and immediately made a beeline for Tyler. The last thing he wanted right then was a stranger with a box of Kleenex. Desperate to avoid her, he scanned the room for an empty corner, found it, and ducked away.

Strange to find himself here in *this* corner. Until a few minutes ago, this was the spot where his mother had maintained her vigil over Amanda. Now Tyler's eyes swept along the length of gray blanket that covered his sister's toes, feet, legs, and torso. At the first glimpse of skin, real skin, Amanda's neck, his eyes snapped closed as if against a dust storm. With tight fists, he rubbed the lids and for a minute lost himself in the tricks of his optic nerve: the fantastic explosions of brightness, the wiggling little shapes like transparent worms under an overturned rock.

Tyler was sixteen years old, certainly no baby, and he knew, of course, about the inevitability of death, how everything eventually dies. Batteries and rosebushes and pet dogs and goldfish. Newly hatched birds fall out of nests. When he was a little kid, he had poked at that kind of death with a stick. Human beings, too. They die every day, every hour. Grandmothers and retired neighbors, that kid in the senior class last year hit by a drunk driver. People die on battlefields in foreign countries. They get blown up in airplanes and die just like old stars do, pieces of them thrown across the sky.

Yes, people die.

He steeled himself, blinked, and looked.

A face. A mouth. A nose. His sister's face. Death. Here it was.

He forced himself to hold his gaze steady and take in the details. The curve of her eyebrow, the light down on her upper lip. What was that on the outside corner of her right eye? A mole no bigger than a period on a page, nothing Tyler would have noticed before.

Only suddenly he realized that he *had* noticed it, not in any deliberate way but in the way he had unconsciously absorbed everything about his sister. Everything. Every day. The way she walked with her feet slightly turned out, how her nostrils flared when she was trying not to laugh. This mole, this tiny dot, was part of the landscape of her face. It wouldn't have been his sister without it.

He heard someone in the room say her name. *Amanda.* Then from someone else, his own name, *Tyler*.

He hesitated, then reached out and ran his index finger across her skin. It was still warm. The mole was too flat and small to even feel, but the knowledge that it was there, that he could still touch it, made goose bumps rise on his arms.

The air closed in; the room tilted.

People die.

Even someone whose voice you can hear when she's not there, can die.

Whose towel you can tell by the smell of her sweat.

Whose socks you have stolen out of her drawer.

Whose sandwiches you have shared.

People die.

Sisters die.

His sister was dead.

He took a stumbling step backward, as if a wave had knocked him loose from the only patch of firm ground beneath his feet. Tyler felt as if he were being pulled out to a vast, cold, and dark ocean from which he might never return. He tried to hold on. He tried to resist but couldn't.

THREE

WITH HER HANDS FOLDED before her, Helen Curry entered room 132 and immediately felt the oppressive air. Several hours had passed since the family had received the horrible news, and the parents had been left alone with their daughter. Thank God the older brother had been whisked out of the room by an aunt.

Helen's arrival went unnoticed, or at least unacknowledged. She watched as the father tilted his head in his ex-wife's direction and they pressed together like dolls with magnets in their foreheads. She couldn't help but wonder what Amanda would have made of this reunion, of her own part in it. A child of divorce, Amanda surely had the fantasy that one day some miracle would erase the distance between her parents and bring them together.

But not this distortion of a miracle.

All Helen's instincts and training told her that she shouldn't even be in the room. Privacy was the very least of what these people deserved. But she knew that if she left and didn't say what she needed to say, didn't ask the question that needed to be asked, it would quickly become too late.

"May I?" she said—and, as one, the parents turned in her direction. She didn't wait for an answer but pulled two chairs closer to the hospital bed, taking a seat in one and gesturing for Robert to take the other. His legs stretched out before him, the left ankle locking gently around Claire's right foot, as if ankle-on-ankle was the only thing holding them to earth.

"This must be so unreal for you," Helen began. "So much information at once. Is there anything I can do to clarify things?"

Robert shook his head.

Claire's face had a dazed look, the confusion of a visitor from another planet. "And you are?"

"I'm the coordinator. From the transplant network." As Helen responded, Claire stared at her moving mouth as if she herself were deaf, her ears accessories, useless things for earrings to dangle from.

Helen could tell that the word *transplant* had not quite registered, so she repeated the explanation. "I'm Helen, from the transplant network. I need to ask you something. Something hard. There's no easy way to do this. So I'm just going to come out and ask. Have you thought about organ donation?"

There it was. A question formed by a breath of air and hanging heavy in the silence. A question that even Helen knew had only one reasonable answer. *Of course they haven't thought about organ donation! What parents of a perfectly healthy fourteen-year-old do?*

"Consider it, please. I hope you will."

Another pulse of silence as the confusion cleared and Claire finally understood exactly what had been asked.

"No!" Her words, fueled by the adrenaline of outrage, couldn't get out fast enough. They were disconnected, wild in panic. "Robert. Amanda. I. No. Organs? Fourteen. No cutting. Look. See her. Cutting? No!"

Robert sprang to his feet, torn equally between two actions: wanting to soothe the mother of his children by wrapping his large frame protectively around her and wanting to smash something.

"Shhh," he said tenderly to Claire. "Nobody is going to do anything you don't want." The next word to Helen—"Nobody!"—was followed with a bang of his fist on a nearby table. "You've got a hell of a lot of nerve. This is our daughter, not some container to be opened and emptied."

Helen bowed her head, not out of regret for her

question—it had to be asked—but to let the man's emotion pass over her. She had been doing this job long enough to know that people reacted in so many different ways, with fear, tears, resignation, silence. She knew not to be afraid of his anger or to take it personally. She even understood how, in some way, it might actually be satisfying. This father finally had someone to rage against, when, in reality, everyone in this tragic situation was blameless.

"Robert, please," Claire said. Her voice softened as quickly as it had flared. "It's okay. I'm okay." To Helen: "So sudden, so . . . maybe . . . if we have more time to let it sink in . . . maybe? . . . No! . . . Oh, I don't know, maybe . . . we just need time."

Time, unfortunately, was the enemy. How could Helen stress the urgency to them? The nurses could keep the oxygen and blood flowing for a while, tricking the organs into thinking the girl was still alive. But eventually, too soon, everything would begin to deteriorate. Helen wanted them to understand that. She answered their few questions as gently, honestly, and succinctly as she could. *Was organ donation compatible with their religion? They were Jewish.*

"Yes," Helen said. "It's considered a blessing."

Would people be able to see Amanda, or would she be too—Claire choked on the word—*scarred?* Helen assured them that no one would be able to tell.

"But what about . . ." Claire paused.

"About what?" Helen prompted.

"A miracle. They happen."

Helen didn't say what she was thinking. There wasn't going to be any miracle for Amanda. But there could be a miracle for someone else. "It's your decision," she said before leaving the room. "What do you think Amanda would have wanted? If you decide yes, please decide soon."

On the other side of town in a nondescript office building in a nondescript room, a computer sat on a desk. No human being at the moment; the data input supervisor was off on his coffee break. No ringing phone. Just a computer that was waiting for a decision to be made.

But if someone were to jump ahead and start the paperwork, it would read like this:

Age of potential donor: 14
Height: 4 feet 11
Weight: 85 pounds

As information entered the computer, a profound shift of identity would begin taking place. Amanda Schecter, beloved daughter, studious ninth-grader, sister, girl who could turn backflips and cartwheels, unique being with her own set of likes, dislikes, secrets, and dreams, would begin changing into something else, something anonymous.

Donor #364 with a list of medical attributes: type O-positive blood, strong liver and kidney function, heart strong, no cancer, no HIV.

And then the computer would spring into action with letters, numbers, and charts filling the screen with accounts of age, weight, blood type, organ function tests, dates of previous surgeries.

Recipient #3478: 36-year-old male, needs lungs
Recipient #63: 17-year-old male, awaiting a liver
Recipient #547: 12-year-old female needs a pancreas
Recipient #5670: 8-year-old female on dialysis, close to renal failure

At the top of the list of potential heart recipients: Recipient #6211: 15-year-old female, 5 feet 4, 115 pounds, AB-positive blood type

Can you picture her? It's not too hard. Pale as snow, tired all the time, terrible circulation, waiting with cold hands, cold everything, for a warm heart.

FOUR

LET'S START WITH THE quick version of my life. When I was born, I almost died and then I didn't and then I got into collecting Beanie Babies and then I gave away all my Beanie Babies and then I had surgery and then I got a whole lot better. That meant I could play some sports. But I got sick again. I was probably over sports anyway. So when I was too sick to do much of anything, I watched lots of TV shows and movies. And I thought about my past. That's what you do when you have too much time on your hands. Think, think, think. I was a regular dwell-on-the-past machine. But then I decided, enough of that! And turned my brain 180 degrees in the other direction.

That's where I am now, contemplating my future.

What about it? What's out there waiting for me?

What if my future's like . . . well, what if it's like that old movie I saw?

Music, please. Opening credits of *Hands of a Stranger*. Sixties haircuts and cars. Enter a young, gifted pianist named Vernon, who is smack in the middle of musical stardom. He's riding high on life, until he's involved in a car accident in which his hands get mangled like dog meat. Next, enter the well-meaning but ethically challenged surgeon who removes Vernon's hands and replaces them with a brand-new pair, courtesy of a fresh corpse.

Since the surgery is bizarrely experimental and has never been performed before anywhere on earth, you can bet that Vernon's insurance company didn't cover the costs.

So anyway . . .

After the surgery, reality sets in quicker than a staph infection, which is something that I hope to never, ever have again in my life. It turns out that Vernon's replacement hands came off the body of a murderer. You know this because the hands were filmed in the kind of creepy black and white that was popular in 1960s low-budget horror films.

It turns out that you can take the hands off a murderer, but you can't take the murderer off the hands.

If I were writing an essay about this movie in standard MLA format, this would be my second paragraph thesis point: *Body parts have a mind of their own.* The new appendages take Vernon down a very dark path indeed. He starts his murderous rampage with an ex-girlfriend who didn't bother to visit him in the hospital; the hands knock her backward over a table, sending romantic candles against the curtains and her whole apartment up in flames.

This last scene isn't as scary as it sounds, despite the spine-chilling musical accompaniment. As Beth— aka Mom—reminds me, moviegoers back in the sixties had a lot less tolerance for serious bloodletting and decapitations than we do today. The murder scene is actually kind of funny, except if you're about eight. My cousin Cara came completely and totally unglued and had to sleep with her mother for the rest of the week. Baby! Guess who got blamed for letting Miss Delicate Nerve Endings watch the sci fi–horror channel?

Me. Moi. Danielle, Dani. That's who.

I won't spoil the ending of the movie because you might be home sick from school one day and wind up watching this horror classic. I thoroughly recommend it. Some people might consider it lame, but where they see cheesy acting and disappointingly tame love scenes, I see a thinking person's medical thriller that turns your brain inside out with questions. Such as:

Is a piano player's life worthwhile if he can't play the piano? In other words, why bother living if you can't follow your passions?

Just how much should medical personnel be mixing and matching body parts?

What makes you *you* and me *me*, besides the standard package of muscles, veins, hair, and organs?

I don't know about people with ordinary medical histories, but I personally can't get enough of this kind of thinking. My history, to put it mildly, is extensive. If you think *you* have problems—period cramps, enlarged skin pores, perhaps a cluster of gross warts on your hand—that's nothing. I'm the belle of the misery ball.

Fifteen years ago, I got taken out of the womb with my heart on the wrong side of my body, the right as opposed to the left. There's a technical name for it, dextrocardia, but I invented my own: Dani's Freakish Feng Shui Chest Cavity.

I could have lived just fine like that. No problem. It was all the other crazy stuff, like screwed-up valves and how messed up the wall separating the two sides of my heart was. Nobody expected me to live long, but I did—long enough to start a whole big stink in seventh grade by putting my left hand over my heart during the Pledge of Allegiance. Certain girls accused me of being unpatriotic. It was very gratifying to hear the president of the Young Patriots Club grovel and apologize when my mom set them straight.

So in all honesty and modesty, I'm kind of a medical-miracle person. Just ask Dr. Emily Alexander or anyone else in the pediatric cardiology department of Children's Hospital. I don't like to publicize myself much because some people might think I'm searching for sympathy, which I'm not. I'm *not*.

But it's not fair. I don't smoke. I don't drink. I'm not some fatty fat. Still my life has been one long science experiment that nobody ever gets entirely right. I've had more X rays, cath lab appointments, treadmill tests, pre-op exams, intravenous drips, and green hospital Jell-O than any smoking, drinking, fatty sixty-year-old man. Not fair. I don't want another surgery.

But what I want and what I need exist in different universes. The whole story is in the mirror. Tired brown eyes. Stringy hair and gray skin. My lips look like I've been sucking on blue lollipops. I look like what I am, a girl who needs oxygen.

I need a new heart.

I don't know why they call it a *new* heart, because it's obviously going to be a previously *used* heart. Used by who? What if I get the heart of a murderous deranged nutcase and it pumps all that evil through my body? Or a boy's heart? A huge, sour-smelling, zit-popping, sweaty-faced boy's heart? That can't be good for a person. Or a five-year-old's heart, a hyper one? How pathetic would that be, now that I've gotten so mature?

But those aren't the questions right now. That's what Mom keeps reminding me. She says to pray that the beeper from the hospital goes off soon. Because a blue-lipped, cold-handed, gray-skinned fifteen-year-old is in no position to turn up her nose at any heart at all.

FIVE

THE HOSPITAL BEEPER DIDN'T go off. I did.

This was not the one-day-this-pain-will-be-good-for-you kind of pain. If you're thinking that your life is too cushy and tame and what you need is some intense suffering to get your character maturing, get your pivotal experience some other way. For instance, go backpacking barefoot in the Andes. Get a piercing like the one my mom got the day she turned eighteen and that she says was one of the most stupid things she ever did in her life. The piercing went straight through the edge of her belly button and out the other side.

But back to that morning. As usual, I was in bed with my pink and orange polka-dotted comforter bought on sale at Target, which Mom pronounces in the fake French way—Tar-*jay*. (That was funny the first time she said it, but not the two-thousandth time.) I was zoned out on a combination of painkillers and TV game shows. I do understand that I'm describing a dream day for many stressed-out, overachieving teens. For me, though, this had become a lifestyle. Most people are nouns; I was a passive verb.

I routinely took diuretics to remove fluid from my body, which—not to sound unladylike or anything—made me pee like Seabiscuit. So at about ten that morning, I needed to go. I *really* needed to go. But I didn't want to call Mom for help. If I called her, we would no doubt wind up having the dreaded bedpan conversation again, which always went something like this:

"Just take it into consideration, Dani. Using a bedpan will let you save energy for what really matters."

"What really matters? Honestly, Beth, what could matter more than getting to pee in the toilet like a normal person?"

"I hate when you call me Beth. I'm Mom."

"I hate when you push the bedpan on me."

"Okay, no bedpan."

"It's a deal, *Mom*."

So as you see, just getting bathroom help meant setting off the whole, exhausting, déjà-vu mother-daughter family dynamic. Which was why on that morning—the morning I'm talking about—I decided not to bother her. I stuck out my tongue at the baby monitor that was always turned on in case of emergencies. I remember moving aside my comforter, my right leg swinging over the edge of the mattress, my foot touching the carpet. I pushed to a seated position and took a minute to gather the strength to stand. I stood.

That's when it hit. Hot. Cold. A sensation like someone had turned on the air-conditioning and space heater full blast at the same time. Then a wave of nausea. A far-off ringing came at me, slammed into the side of my head. I remember pain, pain everywhere.

Then nothing. That was it for remembering.

What I don't remember and learned about only later: My legs buckling and sending me crumpling to the floor hard enough to leave a nasty purple bruise on my forehead. *Lovely*. My hand knocking the monitor off the table. Mom rushing into my room, her voice shouting into the phone. An ambulance screeching up the street. All the nosy neighbors leaving their apartments to see what the fuss was about. EMTs all over me, pounding my chest, breathing what was surely bad breath through a tube into my mouth. Doors slamming, siren blasting, the ambulance running red lights.

Next thing I do remember was blinking open my eyes, and there they all were in a semicircle around me: my very own grim-faced medical cast of hundreds. White-clad figures with stethoscope necklaces came in and out of focus. Like I was at the bottom of a pool and they were looking down at me from the surface. One by one, they leaned in, shapes swirling. Their faces were huge.

Short, grayish hair. Dr. Emily Alexander, pediatric cardiologist.

Bushy, black eyebrows. Cardiac surgeon Dr. Sean McGarry.

Mole with hair sprouting on left cheek. Dr. Jon Bailiff, anesthesiologist.

Brianna V., Monday-through-Friday daytime floor nurse.

Head Nurse Joe.

Dark, wavy hair. Mom.

Dr. Bruce Lubeck, pediatric cardiology second opinion. "Great," he said. "She's back in the world."

Wires, tubes, needles. Something sharp in my chest, pain along my arms and down my throat. "Ugghhh," I groaned.

Truthfully, I'm not sure whether I actually made an *ugghhh* sound, or whether I just had an *ugghhh* thought that never made its way down from my brain, up through my throat, over my tongue, and out into the air where people could actually hear it. I was that out of it. You might think you know what out of it feels like because of certain experimental alcohol or drug use, but you don't know. You *don't*. My eyelids closed.

"Dani? Can you hear me?" Dr. Emily, with her calm-in-any-crisis doctor voice.

Now Mom. "Dani, we're right here. Right next to you." Did she just squeeze my hand?

Dr. Emily again. "Give us a sign, sweetheart. Okay? If you can hear me, let us know. Can you blink for us?"

I felt my eyeballs rolling like pebbles under the lids. But raise the lids? And then lower them again? Blink? She might as well have asked me to jump out of bed and rearrange the furniture.

Touch and go. Once I woke trying to scream "Mom!" and flailed at the wires and tube in my throat. I was in and out of it for days until the doctors finally got me stabilized. Still, I felt bad. I felt bad and headachy and sore all over, like the poor piñata at the end of the birthday party.

"I wish I was dead."

"No you don't. You don't!" Beth—Mom—has this amazing ability to see happy endings everywhere and tried to assure me that the worst was over. "The breathing tube is out."

"Why do they call it a breathing tube when it makes it so hard to breathe?"

"And the fluid pressure around your heart is lower." She stroked my cheek. I think she was trying to rub some color back into it. She picked up my left hand, folded it in hers, and kissed it. "Your hands. They're still so cold."

"Mom, did you have to miss a lot of work? You missed a lot of work. And what about school?"

In addition to being a single mom and working full-time in a boring real estate office *and* trying to sell stuff on eBay, Mom went to school two nights a week at the local community college. She was trying to get into the *exciting, challenging, and financially lucrative career of medical technology.* It didn't exactly feed her creative side, but thanks to my extensive medical history, she had a ridiculous amount of experience in the field.

"Missing a little school? No problem. You know I'm the star of that class. I can afford to take off a few days."

"Beth! You're lying."

"Dani! Don't call your ancient mother a liar."

That last part, the "ancient" part, was Beth being ironic, since she's only seventeen years older than me. Plus, where I'm challenged in the gorgeousness department, Mom is . . . well, every male doctor in the hospital does a double-take when he first lays eyes on her. I can see their minds hoping for a chance to practice a little mouth-to-mouth resuscitation. But she didn't look so ravishing just then. Her hair was matted, her lips chapped. She wasn't going to stop anyone in his tracks, not even the potato-shaped orderly who usually drooled over her. I was about to point this out in a constructive way when Dr. Emily came in to examine me. Mom released my hand and moved aside.

"Hmmmm," Dr. Emily said, stethoscope on my chest.

"Hmmmm good?" Mom asked with hope.

"Hmmmm not so good."

"How much not good?"

Stethoscope off. Worried look on. "Not good at all."

"What are you saying?" Mom asked. "Are you saying she needs more surgery? Surgery will fix this, right?" She glanced at me sideways and lowered her voice to a stage whisper, as if that would protect my delicate ears. "Maybe we should, you know, talk about this first ourselves? Is this a good time for . . . considering what she just went through—"

Dr. Emily placed her hand on Mom's arm. "I know you want to protect her. You are a great advocate, but I think she's old enough to—"

"I'm old enough, Beth."

"To hear about her situation straight. Okay?"

Mom started to protest, but she was outnumbered. She crossed her arms against her chest. Dr. Emily went on, this time directly to me. "Dani, your heart has deteriorated too much. There's no bringing it back anymore. We—all of us—knew this time would come eventually."

She talked on for a while using medical terms, but all I heard was this: I wasn't going anywhere. Definitely not barefoot to the Andes. Not back to school. Not even back home to my pink and orange polka-dotted comforter, which suddenly seemed like heaven.

I wasn't going anywhere, not without a new heart.

And who knew how long that would take? Obviously, a person can't just go to the Major Organ Boutique and order up a perfect heart to go. I knew all about the transplant waiting list. I was already on it. Sometimes just to torture myself, I would Google the words *heart, transplant, list* and up popped the depressing statistics. There were three thousand of us in the country waiting. Each day, eight people on the list died. People *died* from what I had.

"How long can a heart like mine last?" I asked.

"I can't really answer that. Each person is different. Each person is—"

"How long?"

"Worst case scenario? If you don't get a heart in two weeks . . ." Her voice drifted off.

"Two weeks!" Mom blurted out.

"Worst case." Then Dr. Emily actually found something optimistic in all this. "Dani, you've been moved to the very top of the transplant list, from Status 2, somewhat stable, to Status 1A. In dire need."

In my world, that's what passed for great news. First come, first served. I was at the top of the heap.

Top of the messed-up heart heap. Congratulations, Dani.

Beep-beep-beep-beep-beep.

I must have drifted off because a commotion in my room jarred me out of sleep. One of the zillion machines I was hooked up to was having a conniption. *Beep-beep-beep-beep-beep.* I wanted to ignore it and keep sleeping. Sleeping felt so good, the only escape from the constant ache and nausea that ruled my life. But the beeping reached in and hooked on to me. Against my will, I was being yanked down to the surface from the farthest reaches of outer space.

My eyes opened to see a frantic Nurse Brianna tearing into the room. She rushed to my side and examined cords and tubes, looking for kinks and malfunctions, trying to figure out why my IV hookup—the only thing keeping my heart pumping with enough force to keep me alive—signaled distress.

Head Nurse Joe peered into the room. He was one of those people you automatically see as a cartoon animal. Add whiskers and pointy ears and—bingo!—Bugs Bunny. I also considered him to be one of the greatest bald adults who ever lived. He had stories about his own teenage experiences—protest marches, rock concerts, all-night dancing. These are things that I definitely hope to have the heart-lung capacity to experience someday.

"Do you see her?" he asked. "Is she in here? We need to find her. Stat!"

Nurse Brianna tilted her chin in the direction of my IV. "She definitely *was* here. That little one has got the fastest fingers in the West."

Nurse Joe's eyes narrowed and scanned the room, eventually landing on something that made him visibly relax. He put his index finger to his lips in a *shhhh*. "Come on out," he said softly, like he was talking to a cat.

It wasn't a cat. It was a girl scrunched up behind a chair, arms looped around her knees. When she noticed me looking, she covered her mouth in a giggle. I figured she was about six or seven, your basic first-grader except for her hair. A ton of blond curls cascaded down beyond her shoulders. I would have killed for hair like that. Probably some patient's little sister. She flipped all that scrambled-egg hair and giggled again.

Personally, I'm not a big fan of little kids, especially the ultra-adorable ones. Cute is definitely overrated in my opinion. You could already see what this girl was going to be like in middle school, concrete scientific evidence that Queen Bees are born, not made.

Nurse Joe made a lunge—"Gotcha!"—and lifted her from under both armpits. Suspended in midair, her legs whirred, another character in a cartoon.

"Put me down! I'm delicate!"

Nurse Joe headed for the door, trying to talk sense to her. "Honey, this isn't the Touch Museum. You need to leave the buttons alone."

"No touching *me*! Momma doesn't allow it. I'm sensitive! I have a medical condition!"

"Wendy, you're overtired! It's not the end of the world. It's just nap time."

That girl could howl! In my own delicate state, any

noise, especially high-pitched, spoiled-little-girl noise, made even my toes wince. I wouldn't have minded slipping back into a coma right then.

Nurse Joe said over his shoulder to me, "With this kind of lung power, she could sing lead for the Rolling Stones. Hey, I saw the Rolling Stones in their first American concert."

"I know," I said. "Summer 1964."

Nurse Brianna gave him a thumbs-up as he carried the girl out the doorway.

When they were gone, I asked weakly, "Who was that?"

"Wendy. Room 3. Waiting for a kidney. Believe it or not, according to her tests, she's supposed to be just about comatose. You didn't hear this from me. We're supposed to love all our patients just the same. But that one? We love her, but she's driving us crazy."

Nurse Brianna reset my machinery, plumping the IV bag to make sure the liquid flowed smoothly down the tube and into my veins. "Still, you have to give her credit. She's a fighter."

Another howl. Wendy or a cat getting a shampoo?

Lucky me. Meet the neighbor.

SIX

MORE DAYS PASSED IN a blur of sleep, droning TV, prodding and probing by nurses, Mom's worried face in and out of focus, plus the continuing background noise of Wendy fresh from dialysis treatment. Like an old dog, I slept a lot more than I was awake. Days weren't much different than nights.

Gradually, though, the hospital miracle machines did their job. I stayed awake more often, and when I was awake, I didn't just stare into space with drool hardening on the corners of my mouth. Lovely, I know.

The family in the apartment next door to us sent a thousand-piece jigsaw puzzle of a famous painting that I would like to see in person someday because it means a trip to Paris, the city of lights and romance. I worked on the puzzle for a while. Then Beth read aloud the good parts of a trashy novel. We had a laugh over the heavy breathing.

"What if I never get to experience any heavy breathing in my life?"

"Wow," Mom said. "You really must be feeling better, to even consider such a thing."

At least I was feeling a little more like myself. The real sign of improvement was that I was getting bored. I pleaded with Dr. Emily, but she said that I still wasn't strong enough to move around (hello, catheter, which is worse, *much worse,* than a bedpan). For the time being, she also ruled out visitors other than Mom. Human beings are conveyor belts of germs, and I needed to stay as healthy as possible, or at least as healthy as someone who is facing death can be. If a heart became available—a heart that just happened to fit *my* particular chest size and *my* particular blood type—I'd be screwed if I even had the sniffles.

So I was floored when my nurse asked, "How would you like some company?" Nurse Brianna was clearing away my scrumptious breakfast of weak tea and even weaker chicken broth.

"Company? Who? Not Wendy! No way."

"Room 1. Your neighbor on the other side. You have a lot in common."

"What do we have in common?"

"Well, you know." With her right arm, she made a grand sweeping gesture around the hospital room.

Great. Terrific. Other kids my age hook up because

they like the same music or work on the school paper together or find the same things hilarious or have the same plans for the future. I was supposed to hit it off with someone just because they also happened to be screwed in the major organ department. Such was my social life. It was pathetic. But I didn't see any other choice.

"Sure, why not?" I said. "The near-dead are my kind of people."

Right after lunch (more broth and Jell-O), Nurse Brianna pushed in a wheelchair with Nurse Joe guiding a bunch of clinging, clanging equipment. This wasn't what I expected. I assumed my visitor would be a girl, not a boy with yellow skin and green hair. Nice color combination. Plus, there was something scary about him.

Okay, to be perfectly truthful here, there was something scary to me about *any* boy. When you've spent half your life absent from school, you miss out on all the practice opportunities of being around them. Mom was the big dater in our family. I was most comfortable talking to middle-aged doctors about potassium-sparing diuretics. This next confession is even more mortifying: What little social know-how I did possess came by analyzing characters on TV shows like reruns of *Degrassi* (both classic and *Next Generation*). I figured that if I decided which character I most resembled, I'd have my social blueprint for knowing how to talk and act. *Am I the loud and funny girl who is really sensitive inside? The shy one who's really a cutthroat? The smart one who wants to be popular? The popular one who wants to be smart?*

Nurse Brianna backed up the wheelchair and angled the boy in like he was an SUV and I was the curb. Could they possibly manage to bring him any closer?

The whites of the boy's eyes were also yellowish, like he had drunk nothing but orange juice for years. His hair stood up in a punk style. Either that or he slept on it funny. I looked away when he caught me studying him. That was close.

Joe introduced us: "Dani, this is Milo. Milo, Dani. Hey, you two both love music. Awesome, right?"

I still said nothing. Now I knew which sitcom character I was: the one who got cut out of the script. *The seriously lame and pathetic one.*

Suddenly, I was very, very tired. This was not a lie. I repeat: Not a lie! I was exhausted. People waiting for a new heart are allowed to get too tired for visitors, aren't they? It's their right! I definitely didn't want company. Not this *Milo*. What kind of name was that anyway?

But then the nurses left. Just like that, they were gone. Poof, like the evil magicians they were. And it was just me and him. Me in a pink flannel nightgown with a boy I didn't know wearing striped cotton pajamas, the matching kind that usually only grown-ups wear.

I was really grateful when Milo said, "Hey."

"Hey," I said back. I couldn't think of anything to add.

He seemed to be making a serious study of our IV poles, which were lined up side by side and reminded me of two skinny old men, pals from the good old days. "Sixteen," he blurted.

"Excuse me?"

"Sixteen."

I got it. "Oh, I'm fifteen."

"Liver," he said.

"Heart."

Silence again, except for the drone of the machines that were keeping us alive. They were slightly out of sync, beeping and pinging and humming, and came together in a weird, jittery harmony. As Milo studied the poles, I took the opportunity to grab a better look at him. His jaw jutted forward slightly. His nose was straight and strong. He chewed on the inside of his cheeks, which made his face all lines and planes, like a statue of one of our country's Founding Fathers. The young, brilliant, passionate Thomas Jefferson. There was something fierce and dangerous about that. I liked it.

Say something, Dani. "That's good."

"What's good?"

His eager response gave me the confidence to go on. "That you need a liver and I need a heart. That's good. It means we're not in competition. You know, for the same organ? Not in competition."

Milo started doing the chewing thing again, this time with his upper lip. "That *would* suck."

I was trying so hard not to stare at his lips and to think of the next interesting thing to say that I lost the thread of our conversation. "What would suck?"

"What you just said. It would suck if we were both waiting for the same organ. That kind of competition could get ugly."

"Ugly. Right."

"Actually, it would be okay if you needed a liver, too. Two people can use one liver—did you know that?"

I shook my head.

"After they rip it out of some poor guy's dead body, they cut it in half, and after the transplant, both lobes grow to almost full size. Can't do that with a heart, though. Too bad for your sorry ass."

"Yeah, too bad."

He cracked his knuckles. "Twenty-seven bones in the hand, 206 bones in the human body." Then he went back to studying the wall and I was back to studying my lap and trying to come up with another good topic. I went with my sure-fire attention getter.

"My heart. It's on the right side of my body."

"So?"

"Not right as in correct. I mean, the wrong side, which is the right side."

"Cool," he said. "That could come in handy. Like if someone was trying to murder you by stabbing you in the heart with a fork, he'd miss."

Then I remembered some sitcom dating advice: *To break the ice, ask boys about themselves. Something personal. They like that.* "So, what are you anyway?"

"You mean, like what sign? I'm a Gemini. Not that I believe in that. I've definitely ruled out astrology as a life philosophy."

"Not your sign. Your blood type."

"Oh."

"O?"

"No, I'm B. That kind of sucks."

"Not so bad. I'm lucky because I'm AB. Universal receiver. That means—"

"I know what it means! You can get a heart from anyone."

"At least you're not type O."

He brightened at that. I guess I passed some kind of private test of medical knowledge. He got the nicest smile creases around the corners of his mouth. For the first time, he looked directly at me, like he had completely forgotten to be embarrassed about having orange horror-film eyes. His eyeballs themselves were normal green. Normal with flecks of brown, like little sparks, scattered through them. As eyeballs go, they were extremely attractive ones.

"Yeah, type O can only take from another O. That's fucked up," he said.

"Not for some people. Universal donor! An O can give an organ or blood to anyone, save lots of lives."

"I'm not in any position to be giving. You either."

"Obviously. So, how long have you been waiting?"

"Just a couple of weeks this time."

"This time?"

"Yeah. I'm on my second transplant. The first one I got when I was three. This is Liver Transplant, take two. Liver Transplant: The Sequel. Liver Transplant: The Next Generation."

"Son of Liver Transplant. What happened to the first one?"

"Crashed and burned. Guess I had something to do with that. Long story."

Milo slumped a little and I have to say that he looked really good doing it. Not everyone has enough personal style to get away with poor posture. When he mumbled something, I didn't catch the words.

"I'm sorry. I—"

"Don't! Don't ever feel sorry for me! It's the way it is."

"I'm not sorry for you. I just didn't hear what you said."

He went on as if I hadn't explained. "I'm sick of people and how they get all weird and sorry for me. I'm not sorry for me. Since I made the most-likely-to-die list, I've gotten philosophical. I'm making a study of it."

"It?"

"Everything. Everything that's important to know. Death, life, what it all means. All the world's belief systems, past and present. Hedonism. Hinduism. Rastafarianism. Existentialism." He ran his nails through his hair, gave his head a hard scratch. "Yeah, I used to be into the whole darkness-of-the-soul thing. For a while, I was a nihilist. You can tell by my hair. Right now, I'm digging deep into the secret society of the Rosicrucians."

Secret society? I wanted to ask about that. I also wanted to ask what he meant by *having something to do* with needing a second transplant. There was no opportunity because Brianna, all nursey and chirpy, stuck her head in the door. "Okay, you two. Visiting time is over. Nice chat?"

Neither of us answered. As the nurse wheeled him out the door, Milo flashed the peace symbol over his shoulder.

Meet the neighbor, part two. Scary, but definitely better than Wendy.

After that major social interaction, I fell asleep. I woke up in time for dinner, and as I waited for it to arrive, I decided that it would be a good idea to know more about philosophy. My education was definitely sketchy in that area. Rastafarian? That had something to do with dreadlocks and smoking pot, didn't it? Existentialism? Something about being French and living in a world that was mad and out of your control. I could definitely use advice on that.

By the time my delicious meal of semisolids (coddled egg and applesauce) arrived, I decided that Milo was okay, better than okay. Certain girls in school would say *ewww* about his skin color and death talk. But at least he didn't have too many zits. And maybe, I thought, maybe he would be really hot with a new haircut and a new liver.

As I played with my food, my mind drifted. *What did Milo think of me? What did I look like through his eyes? Could he make out any facial beauty beyond my pasty skin? Did he think I had a scrawny chicken neck? Did he think I was cute at all?*

And what did he think of my ability to hold an interesting conversation? Did he think I was worth talking to again? I didn't say anything stupid, did I? Did I say something stupid? I don't think I did. Did I? Would he ask to visit me again? When? Tomorrow? What if he didn't ask? Should I ask the nurse about a visit if he doesn't ask first? Would that be too pushy? Some boys on TV shows like pushy girls. Maybe Milo does.

All this wondering made my heart speed up. I could feel it pumping. Not good. It was supposed to be beating at a nice, even pace. I wasn't supposed to let anything bother my peace of mind.

So did he think I was nice at least? Being nice wasn't a bad thing to be. No, nice was awful. The worst. Nice was coddled eggs and applesauce. Nice was totally bland and forgettable.

What was wrong with me anyway? I was chronically ill, this close to death. I should have been thinking about getting a new heart and what would happen if I didn't get it. I should have been wondering about the meaning of my short life and how cheated I'd feel if fifteen was *it* for me.

I should have been thinking about that.

But I wasn't.

So maybe I was mentally ill on top of every other kind of ill. Because, truthfully, all I could think about was that boy.

Dark. Clicking and beeping. Lights somewhere off in the distance. Humming electrical sounds. The rattle of something rolling. A cart? A voice over a speaker jarring me awake.

Where was I?

Night hospital sounds. That's right. I remembered.

My body felt unattached to me, a thing lying there while I hovered above it. These must be *some* new drugs that were pumping through my veins. I saw my own head, nose, eyes, arms, legs. I was alone in the hospital room, but I heard numbers whispered at me. Something in my own mind whispering to itself. The number 206. What did *that* mean?

Oh! That's the number of bones in the human body. My body. Everyone's body.

Two people, 412 bones. Two people, two faces, two noses, four eyes, four ears, eight limbs, two livers that can grow into four, four kidneys, ten liters of blood, 1,300 muscles, 120,000 miles of blood vessels, 200,000 hairs on two heads.

Two people, two hearts. But only one of them working.

I want that heart.

I won't be picky. I'll take the first one that comes along.

I want to be normal and go to school and cut PE classes.

I want a boyfriend and a trip to Paris.

I want to sit in a café and drink coffee and argue about movies.

I want to pierce my ears.

I want to eat salty pretzels and fried calamari rings.

I want to live to be an old lady with deep wrinkles who wears purple and half scares the neighborhood kids.

I want a new heart.

Later that night, another thought, a disturbing half dream.

Everyone keeps talking about finding a heart for me, as though one were hidden behind the couch in a game of hide-and-seek, or it had been misplaced along with someone's cell phone. But that's not how it works. I know that. Even if no one talks about it.

If a heart is found for me, it means that somebody else, some mother, some father, some kid, somebody who is in perfect health—except for being dead—has just lost everything.

SEVEN

WHY DID THEY KEEP bothering him? Didn't they *get* what the lock on his bedroom door meant? Couldn't they understand the meaning of the yellow police banner that he taped in an *X* across his closed door? Off-limits. Caution. Do not cross.

Do. Not. Cross.

Still, every hour Tyler heard footsteps coming up the stairs. He had lived in this house his whole life, so he knew exactly how long it would take them to reach his door. The hollow thud as they left the carpeted stairs and hit the hardwood landing, the squeak of the floorboard as they passed his sister's room. Tyler felt powerless to stop them.

From the chair at his desk, he watched the band of sunlight from the hallway disappear from the bottom crack of his door. He could see the tips of shoes side by side. There was never a knock right away. No, they had to just stand there waiting. Sucking all the air out of his room. What did they think he was doing in here? Sobbing hysterically? Designing plans to blow up a building? Writing a suicide note?

An hour earlier, there had been three firm raps, his father's signature knock. Tyler inhaled and with his exhalation came the expected series of soft, rapid taps. Mom's turn to check up.

"Tyler, are you okay in there? Just answer me, please. Are you hungry?"

"No."

"But, honey, you haven't eaten since yesterday. How about a sandwich? I can make you something."

Without inflection: "No."

"How about a banana?"

A banana? Why did they keep offering him bananas? Why would he want a banana?

"Tyler, it isn't good shutting yourself off. Do you want to talk?"

"No."

Silence.

But silence is never really silence, is it? Tyler could hear the whooshing sound of his own blood in his ears. And even when his parents weren't talking, it was as if their voices had burrowed into his brain and wouldn't shut up. His mind created dead-on imitations. His mother's thin voice, dripping with too much concern: *Tyler, honey, do you want a hug?* His father's voice, so manly casual on the surface, but just as intrusive: *Hey, son, how's about you and me getting a little fresh air?*

"Go away."

And still his mother's shoes didn't move. He pictured her standing in the hallway, all those new lines in her forehead that had appeared suddenly the day before. That day. *The* day. Was it only one day ago? The day everything changed.

An image—the last time he had seen his sister alive—flashed through his mind. Amanda in her room, cross-legged on her bed, looking up at him as he entered. The looks of annoyance ricocheted between them. Tyler shook away the memory.

"Mom, I'm okay. Really. I'm just doing homework. Go away."

He waited for something more from the other side of the door—a challenge, a bribe, a plea—but nothing came. The sunlight reclaimed the place of the shoes. Relief. When the footfalls reached the bottom of the stairs, it felt like he and his parents were not only on different floors, but in different universes. It was only then that Tyler felt he could breathe again.

He turned his attention back to his laptop. The screensaver had popped on. It was a colorful swirling bundle of digital twine that spun and twisted around the screen. Tyler put his concentration there and let himself get sucked into the motion. There were so many variables under his control with a click on the touchpad. What would it look like if he increased the speed? Changed the colors? Altered the shape of the loops? It seemed very important right then to know everything about the screensaver, to get it exactly the way he wanted it.

There. That was perfect. But what now?

Of course he had no intention of doing homework like he had told his mother. He only said that in hopes that it would make her go away sooner, since she was a total control freak about it. *Tyler, did you do your math? Tyler, do you remember you have to start that SAT prep class?* He hated homework because it was bullshit and because he was ordered to do it. He had always been that way with anything mandatory. Meals and bedtime and chores and standing in straight lines and tests and clothing and politeness. Something just clicked inside—Tyler could actually feel it snapping in his brain—and he would *have* to do the exact opposite of what was being ordered or asked or expected. How many parent-teacher conferences had been held on the topic of *Tyler's stubborn refusal to get with the educational program*? He just couldn't understand people who didn't have that click of opposition. People who climbed into bed whether they were tired or not, who cleaned their rooms whenever ordered. People like his sister.

Amanda the Perfect.

With no particular intention, Tyler Googled *Amanda* and clicked on a site about the derivation of names.

Amanda. Latin origin. Worthy of being loved.

Perfect. The perfect name for the perfect girl.

He typed again. *Tyler. Old English. A tile maker.*

Why did his parents pick that name for him? A tile maker? The strangeness of it, how different in substance and feeling it was from his sister's name, struck him as hilarious. Hilarious in that dark, cynical Tyler way. Why hadn't they called him—*click on the computer*—Aaron, which means exalted and strong? Or Ari, which means lion? Or Sam, "His name is God"? Of all the names in the world, his parents chose *Tyler.* They might as well have named him Hammerholder or Bricklayer.

An old, familiar chill of jealousy rushed through his body. He actually shivered with it. With his right hand, he made a fist. He wanted to hit something. Only in the next instant, he remembered that there was nothing to lash out against. Nothing. Not anymore.

All that day, Claire and Robert considered the question the woman from the transplant network had put before them, weighing the two possibilities. Yes or no. Donate or don't donate. *What would Amanda want?* What did they know about their daughter—her character traits, her belief system, her sense of her own body—that would let them make this decision for her?

Robert let his mind wander through memories. Maybe something Amanda once said, an off-the-cuff remark that could be turned into a clue, then followed to a decision. Claire wondered how she could have carried her daughter for nine months, given birth, and lived with her for fourteen years but still not know how to speak for her. She made a silent plea to God, to the position of the planets, to the crack in the universe, to whatever force produces miracles. She wanted one more conversation with her daughter to ask all the questions she had lost the chance to ask: What's your first memory? What do you think about before going to sleep? Donate or not donate?

What would Amanda want?

For Tyler, too, the day stretched and squeezed. Time was as unreal as anything in a fantasy story where past and future slip into the present, where everything is strangely unsolid. In the middle of the night, he gave up trying to sleep and sat in front of the computer, typing words and phrases that randomly came to mind and passed unfiltered to his fingertips.

Heart. In an average lifetime, it beats more than two and a half billion times, without ever pausing to rest.

An average lifetime. Amanda's had been so much shorter than that.

On a medical Web site, a rendering of the brain looked exactly like the bike helmets that his parents always insisted he and Amanda wear. *No helmet, no ride, no argument.* Even the colors of the drawing were bright and kidlike—swirls of purple, silver, yellow, and green— each representing a different section of the brain.

The brain, Tyler read, *is the center of intelligence. It controls behavior.*

Click. *The brain is like a group of specialists.*

Interactive arrows pointed to the various sections. Tyler clicked on each and took his time with the descriptions, sometimes reading them twice before the information sank in. He learned about the oldest parts of the brain that keep the heart beating, the lungs inflating, eyes blinking, food digesting. The cerebellum, which resembles a crumpled tissue, controls muscles and movements you learn by rote.

Tyler moved the mouse and clicked on the various lobes of the cerebrum. These were the more evolved parts of the brain that hold memories, let you enjoy the taste of ice cream and the sound of music, allow you to play games, read books, make up stories, and have impassioned arguments.

Amanda loves music.

Amanda loves reading.

Amanda loves chocolate-chip-cookie-dough ice cream.

Amanda and I sure get into some fights.

Tyler read to himself: *A healthy brain functions rapidly and automatically. But an injury can throw everything into chaos.*

He understood something now, and it was the opposite of the daze and shock he had been feeling all day. He ran his hand through his hair and felt the clarity radiating through every strand.

When the brain is dead, there is nothing left. Not the part that lets you do backflips on a balance beam or enjoy chocolate-chip-cookie-dough ice cream. Not the part that lets you fight with your brother or even recognize the members of your family. Not the part that lets you plan for the future. Because there is no future. You can't even blink your eyes.

Tyler typed: *If you really care what I think, here it is. Brain-dead isn't something you* have, *like a disease that can be cured. Brain-dead is something that you* are.

He printed it out and slipped the paper under his mother's bedroom door.

EIGHT

In the morning, when Tyler's parents didn't get an answer to their knocks, they used one of Amanda's bobby pins to pop the lock on his bedroom door. Tyler was sound asleep, his left cheek pressed against one pillow, a second pillow balled up and held against his stomach. They decided not to wake him and tiptoed away from his door, leaving a note on the floor where he couldn't miss it.

At ten, he woke up. His head hurt; his stomach ached. An emotional hangover felt worse than anything caused by cheap vodka. He didn't want to be feeling any of this. It wasn't fair. Groggy, sitting up, he sniffed hard and tasted the phlegm that had built up in his sinuses overnight. Hacking it up, he spit the gob into a wastebasket. When he headed for the bathroom, he stepped on the note before seeing it.

Dear Tyler,
Your dad and I decided to let you sleep while
we returned to the hospital. You know that we
had an important decision to make today. After
we read your thoughts, we decided to go ahead
and allow the organs to be used for transplant.
We don't know if we're doing the right . . .

The note went on a little longer, but Tyler crumpled it into a ball, tossed, watched the arc, and pumped his fist in the air when it landed successfully in the trash can. In the bathroom, he peed, brushed his teeth, as usual didn't bother to floss, then splashed cold water on his face.

What now? Now what?

Tyler usually liked having the house to himself. He actually lived for the rare times when his mother had an after-school meeting or those long, precious Sundays—six A.M. until way after dark—when everyone was away at a gym meet and he could raid the refrigerator, maybe even smoke a little pot. But this empty house felt different, more empty than empty. He took two steps in the direction of the stairs, then two more. At the entrance to Amanda's room, he stopped. If anyone had been watching, they would have thought that he was practicing to be a street mime bumping up against an invisible pane of glass.

The door to Amanda's room looked as it always

looked—no music poster, no KEEP OUT sign, no finger-print smudges on the doorjamb. He tried to keep walking, but something held him there. He felt himself drawn toward the room but repelled at the same time, fascinated at the prospect of entering and also freaked out by it.

With three quick steps, Tyler willed himself over the threshold. He blinked once, twice, before he could hold his eyes steady enough to take it all in.

The walls were bright yellow, the carpet tan. As usual.

The bed was made, the sheets with the pattern of bright orange flowers tucked in at the corners, the pillows plumped. As usual.

Her gymnastics trophies stood lined up, soldiers at attention, on a shelf over her desk. The room was as it always was.

Shouldn't something be different about it? Shouldn't something have changed?

Something had. Something was missing.

Amanda, of course. Amanda at her desk. Amanda on her bed. Amanda looking up at him in complete annoyance, like the last time he had seen her in this room. They had yelled at each other. What else was new? They were always yelling at each other about something, except for when they made vows to not talk to each other at all.

This most recent fight? What had it been about this time?

Tyler remembered something stupid about a DVD. Someone hadn't returned it to the rental store and now the fees were piling up and their mom was mad and Amanda said that Tyler had it last and Tyler said that Amanda had it last and nobody knew where it was. Then Amanda yelled that Tyler was always losing everything, and Tyler came back with some prime sarcasm about how Little Miss Perfect never did anything wrong.

"Stop the blame game," their mother had shouted up the stairs. "Just find the damn movie."

It was Amanda who said the next thing. Tyler was almost positive of that. Yeah, positive. She was always trying to get in the last word. Maybe he *had* called her a dweeb. Yeah, that was something he would say. Or an idiot. Or a jerk. But he was pretty sure that it was Amanda who had yelled out the final insult.

Tyler now began pacing the room, slowly at first, but gathering speed until he was storming around, replaying all the juicy details of their last fight—what he said, what she said, what he said back. He recreated all the hot emotion, repeating the story again and again until he was sure he had remembered it absolutely right.

Until in the story, Amanda had been the one to call him "brain-dead!" And not vice versa.

NINE

NANCY, THE NURSE FROM the transplant organization, tried not to think about what the family of this girl must be doing tonight, what they would be feeling or not feeling, how they were probably preparing for the funeral.

She didn't want to think about that.

How at some point in the long, unreal day, the parents must have taken their first awful step into their daughter's bedroom, opened her closet, and tried to decide how to dress her for burial.

How the mother probably scrutinized each individual item of clothing, because, even though it was completely irrational, she was thinking, *Something warm. I don't want her being cold.*

Nancy pulled her mind back from going off in that direction. Emotionally, she couldn't afford to go there.

Rather, she focused on the work ahead of her that

evening in the intensive care unit. She was a member of the Transplant Donor Network Procurement team. Her official job title, donor management, made what she did for a living sound so insignificant and impersonal, like slapping a new coat of white paint on an apartment wall or shuffling paper. Donor management didn't capture her job at all. She would have preferred to hear it described for what it was: tricking death. Like some wily coyote in one of the folk stories that her son liked to read, or maybe Road Runner in the old cartoons, who always knew just when and how to sidestep what seemed to be certain death. What Nancy would be doing all that night was to fool the body into thinking that it was still alive.

On machines on both sides of the bed, the girl's vital statistics scrolled across screens: oxygen ratios, pulse, blood volume. Nancy was taking the place of a brain that no longer functioned. She fussed over a set of intravenous drips, releasing the right amount of antidiuretics, thyroid hormones, antibiotics, steroids to calm the heart and give it a chance to recover from its near-death experience.

Without this delicate balance of solids, fluids, and gases, how quickly everything would fall apart. Potassium levels would drop, and salt would build up, opening the gates for fluids to pour out of cells. Sugar would quickly build up in the blood. The heart would grow twitchy and irritable, ripe for cardiac arrest. With the pituitary system off-line, the muscles would fill with lactic acid and go as limp as the legs of an exhausted marathon runner. Next to arrive would be a parade of unstable, highly reactive molecules called free radicals. Even though she was a medical professional, Nancy couldn't *not* imagine these molecules as wild, dangerous bearded men who rampaged unchecked through the body.

Her job was about preventing this irreversible march to chaos, to keep the heart and liver and lungs and kidneys alive until the last possible minute before the surgeons were ready to remove them for transplant. Her job in the ICU that night was to worry, fuss, and keep this dead girl as healthy as a live one.

It was going to be a busy night, not just for Nancy, but for the nurses and doctors attending others. A man burned in a car crash moaned constantly, and a woman with advanced lung cancer struggled to breathe. A woman brought in hemorrhaging was on the cusp of bleeding to death. As far as outward appearance, Nancy's charge was far and away in the best shape of them all, as if she didn't even belong in the same wing as such desperately ill patients.

In her years in this job, Nancy had come to think of each one of her cases not as a cadaver or a body, but as a patient—many patients, really, a patient heart, two patient lungs, two patient kidneys. What she wanted was what all nurses want, for her patients to live.

So all night, in her lookout for declining function, she checked blood pressure, urine output, heart rhythms, and oxygen saturation. Over the chest, she placed a vest that was wired to gently shake her patient. Then Nancy, taking the place of a cough, suctioned out the loosened phlegm before it pooled in the lungs.

At 3:30 A.M., just as the nurse picked up a magazine to glance through, a lab tech called, alerting her to a drop in calcium level. To mimic the function of the now-shutdown parathyroid gland, Nancy added calcium to the intravenous drip, and the body responded positively. "Good, good," she said.

At 5:30, as Nancy made a minor adjustment to the ventilator, something made her jump backward. She almost sent the IV pole toppling to the floor. In awe, she watched the arms of her patient slowly stretch out, cross against the chest, and then drop with a chilling finality alongside the torso.

It was the Lazarus sign, a primitive spinal reflex unconnected to the brain, to life, to any kind of hope. Nancy had been trained to expect this medical phenomenon. But how could anyone really be prepared for such a sight? It was always a shock. Her inhalation remained high and tight in her chest until she remembered to breathe.

In early morning as her shift was about to end, the transplant team arrived, filling the room with new energy, like four fully charged batteries. The surgeons knew that once outside the body, a heart can only survive two to four hours at most, a liver six to eight hours, the more hearty kidneys up to twenty-four hours. So overnight while the nurse had been staving off death, they took care of all the prep work, lining up potential matches, performing blood tests, ruling out some recipients and preparing others for transplant.

The lead heart surgeon patted Nancy on the back and told her, "Good job. We've found homes for all the organs."

As she gathered her things to leave, Nancy admitted to herself that she had grown more attached to this patient than she liked to. There was something so vulnerable about the girl, her muscular yet thin arms and the soft down on the sides of both cheeks. She made a silent apology. If only she really did have the ability to trick death. But her powers, even backed by millions of dollars' worth of high-tech medical equipment, were small, laughable, inadequate.

Nancy wanted to do something dramatic then, make some kind of protest about the unfairness of this girl's short life. But what to do?

She said good-bye by touching the girl's right hand. Amanda's hand. It was only slightly cooler than her own.

TEN

Heart surgeon dr. sean McGarry always liked a soundtrack while working. Music piped into the OR kept him focused and calm. Lately, he had a taste for opera. His choice this day was *Carmen*, the tragedy that ends with a jilted lover with bloody hands sobbing over a young woman's body. The other staff had definitely preferred Dr. McGarry's classic rock phase. Pink Floyd for the routine operations and mellow Van Morrison when things promised to be trickier.

This surgery started like so many others. A nurse placed a blanket over the patient's legs and tucked the arms against her sides. She painted on the antiseptic, neck to thigh, a guard against infection, before applying a sterile blue drape with a hole over the chest and abdomen. The anesthesiologist went to work. Even without a functioning brain, spinal reflexes can cause a body to buck in surgery.

A new resident had the honors of opening the abdomen. Nervous but grateful for the opportunity, she used a pencil-like electrocautery instrument to cut from the sternum to below the belly button. A burning smell immediately filled the room. To the veteran staff, it was a familiar scent, but one that nobody ever really got used to. It could be tasted at the back of the throat and made its way to the pit of the stomach. The resident gagged slightly.

The head abdominal surgeon then cut through skin, fat, and a dense web of connective tissue. A retractor held open the strong rectus abdominal muscles. He plunged in his hands, the cut edge of the dermis—the thick pearly white layer between the fat and the outer skin—tightening like elastic around his forearm. He lifted the intestines, setting them aside outside the body.

As always, the abdomen was difficult to navigate through, all those organs crowded into a tiny space. If the belly were a room, there wouldn't be an inch to spare. But the doctor's fingers, knowing their destination, moved with confidence among the spongy organs, looking and feeling for cysts or too much fat. The aorta pulsed against his palm.

"The liver," the surgeon announced. "Smooth, pink, with sharp edges. Looks great."

Someone called the transplant center with the good news.

Through the loudspeaker, tenor Plácido Domingo sang in French, "This flower that you threw to me." A blood pressure monitor beeped to an entirely different rhythm.

Now it was time for Dr. McGarry to open the chest and take his look. The anesthesiologist stopped the ventilator, causing the lungs to deflate temporarily, like a breath held out. The saw buzzed, dropping slightly in pitch as it cut through bone. A retractor held the chest open. The exposed heart beat back and forth like a small animal that had been chased and was breathing hard, cornered in a cave of strange red rock.

Dr. McGarry ran his fingers down the arteries. The heart looked good. The lungs looked good. More good news for the transplant center.

Now all the doctors leaned in and crowded around the patient, cutting off tendons and nerves, tying off any blood vessels that weren't necessary.

Finally. The big event. "Ready to cross-clamp," Dr. McGarry announced.

He clamped the aorta and snipped across the vena cava. "Eleven thirty-nine A.M.," he called out. This was when the clock started ticking for the lifespan of the organs. The anesthesia stopped. The ventilator stopped.

The music from *Carmen* continued:

L'oiseau que tu croyais surprendre.... The bird you thought you had caught beat its wings and flew away.

Bright red blood from the chest and abdomen drained into tubing connected to canisters on the OR floor. The organs were flushed with a cold preservation solution.

The heart came out first. Dr. McGarry pronounced it first rate as he put it into a sterile plastic jar and then double-bagged it in plastic. He handed the bundle to a nurse who placed it into a blue picnic cooler filled with cubes from the hospital cafeteria ice maker.

Sometimes lungs come out a boggy, unusable mess. These were inflated like a set of fluffy pink pillows.

Within the hour, the other organs were removed. The liver, flat and shiny, resembled a river-polished rock. The kidneys and pancreas were packed into clear plastic jars with screw-top lids to protect them from damage during transport.

Carmen and Don José sang *C'est toi? C'est moi*. Is it you? It is me.

It was left then to the new resident to finish up. She gently put the whorl of intestines back into the belly. While closing up the body, she thought about how interesting the heart is. How it both pumps and secretes. How it is electrical and mechanical. How it is, at once, a basic machine and a monumental mystery. She took her time sewing. Only a few people would ever see her work, but she wanted to leave stitches that were as tiny, even, and perfect as humanly possible.

Not long after that, a nurse switched off everything—the monitors, lights, and finally the music. By all accounts, the surgery on Donor #364 was a success.

ELEVEN

"HEY, YOU!"

I was startled out of sleep.

"You, big girl. With the rotten old heart."

I felt myself blinking into the dark with a spaced-out expression. At the foot of my bed, a silhouette began taking shape. Arms, legs, head, hair. Lots of hair.

Wendy.

I bolted upright, ready to defend the only thing standing between me and certain death. In a computer voice, I ordered, "Step away from the IV. Step away from the IV." I pointed an accusing finger at her. "If you get any closer to those buttons, I'll . . . I'll call out the monster under my bed and he'll use you as sandwich meat."

Wendy was wearing pajamas that consisted of frilly pink pants and the kind of skimpy white top that girls my age wear in size extra small when they're going for the slutty look. The word *princess*, the perfect clothing statement for Wendy, was written on it. In her right hand, she clutched a stuffed bunny by one long ear, like she had just nabbed it trying to escape. "I'm not scared of any monster. He'll take one bite and spit me out because I have a dirty old, rotten kidney." She scowled at me. "I don't believe you anyway. Mommy says there are no monsters."

I switched on the nightstand lamp. "Your mother is only familiar with the nonexistence of house-inhabiting monsters. She obviously doesn't know squat about the vicious species that lives under hospital beds."

Wendy's eyes widened for a moment, but only a moment. She stuck out her tongue. For a little kid with a failing kidney, she was pretty sharp, I had to give her that. I did notice, though, that she didn't come any closer to the IV pole. In that totally random little-kid way, she changed the subject. "I took ballet before my kidney turned so rotten." She jumped her feet apart and started sinking into the splits. I guess she was trying to impress me with her phenomenal flexibility, which wasn't so very much since she collapsed forward and hit the floor.

"Who's your best friend?" she asked and didn't wait for my answer. "I have two. My best friends are Rachel and Rachel."

"Doesn't that get confusing?"

"What?"

"That they have the same name. Do you call them Rachel One and Rachel Two? Or Rachel and Rach? Or Chel and Rach?"

"Siiiiilly!" She gave the word five vowels. "I say, 'Hi, Rachel,' and she says, 'Hi, Wendy,' and then I say, 'Hi, Rachel,' and *she* says, 'Hi, Wendy.'"

"Oh." Fascinating.

"What's the name of your heart?"

When I didn't answer immediately because, *pardon me*, I wasn't sure that I heard the question right, she repeated it, this time with an annoying period after each word. "What's. the. name. of. your. heart?"

"A heart doesn't have a name." I said this despite knowing that there wasn't much use arguing because rational thought doesn't work with an age group that still half believes in monsters under beds and fully believes that parents know everything about every-thing, and other insane thoughts like that. I honestly believe that anyone under the age of eleven basically qualifies as being mentally ill.

"Siiiiilly. Of course your heart has a name. The name of my dirty old, rotten kidney is Captain Ga-ga."

"How do you know that?"

"Siiiiilly! He told me."

"Your kidney talks to you?"

"Yeah, in dirty old, rotten pirate talk. He says—"

"That makes no sense—"

"It does!"

"Let me finish! It makes no sense that your kidney is of the male gender, since your kidney is part of you, came from you, and is, genetically speaking, the same as you. Your kidney would have to be a girl, too."

"A girl? No!" Pause. "Are there girl pirates?"

I had her now. "How do you think all the little baby pirates come into the world?"

"How do they?" Pause and a giggle. "Oh, I get it. Mommy pirates."

It felt gratifying to win this argument, like I had shined the light on a very dark corner of someone's mind. Only, what argument had I really won? From outside in the hallway, I heard Nurse Joe's voice—"Wendy!"—and the girl with the pirate kidney took off.

Neighbor #1 has got to be one of the strangest people I've ever met.

Early morning thought:

Fact: Cells are constantly dying, and new ones are taking their place.

Fact: Every second, fifty million of my cells die.

Fact: After seven years have gone by, every cell in my body has died and a new one has taken its place.

Do the math. That means that every seven years, I'm a totally new me. Not one of the old cells remains. Twice, I've had a total makeover.

So how does my body know not to put my nose where my eyes were? And why haven't my cells organized themselves into a proper heart that sits on the proper side of my chest?

If every cell in my body has changed, if nothing is the same as it was, what holds me together? What is it that keeps me being me?

Early afternoon thought:

Let's say that my heart did have a name—it's absolutely ridiculous to consider such a thing, but if it did—what would it be?

Late afternoon thought:

I have a strange feeling. I ride it out to the end. If I had to name it, I'd call it, what? Not love. Definitely not that. A crush. I'm completely crushed on Neighbor #2, swamped with fantasies of my lips meeting his in an explosive human volcanic reaction like when vinegar mixes with baking soda in a science fair project.

Fact: The previous thought doesn't mean that I'm completely boy-obsessed and shallow. I spend a lot of time dwelling on what a girl who is *this close* to death would obviously dwell on. The Big Stuff, like the tragedy of the human condition and the age-old riddle of what happens to us after death.

That's where Milo came in again. Was it mere coincidence that we wound up as next-door neighbors in Children's Hospital?

No. This was destiny and not just because Milo happened to have those sexy crinkles around his mouth. He could provide answers. Before I had a chance to wimp out, I ordered my hand to pick up the receiver and punched in Milo's room number. When his phone rang, my toes did a weird thing. They curled. Under the blanket, my feet played with each other.

A voice on the other end of the phone said, "'Sup?" and I put a throaty shiver into my voice so it sounded more womanly and mysterious. "Guess who?"

"Someone with a sore throat?"

I ignored that. "It's moi. Dani."

"Dani? Oh, yeah, the girl next door."

There was a cough, and I figured that since I could hear that without the phone, his bed sat right up against the wall, a mere few inches of Sheetrock separating us. Our heads were almost touching. We were practically sharing a pillow. That was almost more than I could bear to think about.

"So, hi," I said.

He cleared his throat again and asked why I had called, and I told him I wanted to know how he was feeling, and there was a more important reason why I called.

"Not that how you're feeling isn't important."

"But this more important reason is?"

"I've been thinking about what you said."

"What I said about what?"

"How you're studying different philosophies, things that people believe in. Life, rituals, meaning, birth—"

"Death. That's what I'm interested in. Stiff City, kick the bucket, Adios Park, human roadkill, bite the dust, pay the piper. The big D. The big sleep. Worm food, decay buffet, organic rot fest."

I don't have much firsthand experience about the mating rituals of modern boys, but I could tell that Milo wasn't giving this his romantic all. It was more like he was baiting me, trying to get me to call him sick and perverted, which is what I suppose the less bedridden girls of his acquaintance would have done. But I remained unshocked. Actually I giggled, totally inappropriate, but I guess that's because nervousness and laughter are very closely related in the brain.

"What's so funny?"

For once, I thought of an interesting comeback— not ten minutes after I hung up the phone, but right when I was supposed to say it. "Cowards die many times before their death. Shakespeare said that. My heart may be screwed up, but I have a strong stomach. I really do want to know everything you know about death."

There was silence on the other end. I could tell that Milo wasn't totally convinced yet. He was seriously weighing my sincerity. "The Grim Reaper. Termination Station," I added as encouragement.

Through the receiver, I heard his bed creak, then a little groan of effort. "Getting my notebook on the floor," he explained. "The Complete Journal of Death Through the Ages." The sound of pages turning.

The first thing Milo read aloud was the end of *my* Shakespeare quote. How's that for a connection? "The valiant never taste of death but once." That was followed by more pages turning, and then an apology about his lack of organization. In my opinion, an apology wasn't at all necessary, but it did show me that Milo was a very thoughtful person.

"My research doesn't follow any time line or anything. It kind of meanders all over the death-and-dying spectrum."

"Don't sweat it," I said, and immediately regretted using a phrase that might make him think about armpits and BO. I quickly covered with, "Please, just start anywhere."

"Might as well jump right into your basic Christian philosophy. You probably know this already, but for them, death boils down to a heaven-or-hell fixation. Life is one big test of pain and temptation, where you have to prove yourself worthy of getting into God's playground." He snorted with contempt, then skipped to the Rosicrucians.

"That's the super-secret sect I told you about before. They say that at the moment of death, you strip off your body and throw it away like some old clothes that you don't need anymore." He moved on to ancient Egypt. "The Egyptians believed that to get to the after-life you pass through a dangerous place with monsters, boiling lakes, fires, and some nasty snakes that spit out poison."

I didn't interrupt and say something stupid, like, "Shut up! Have they been watching *Indiana Jones*, or what?" I credit my silence with giving Milo the confidence to go on. Clearly, a relaxed Milo was a talkative Milo.

"The Hindus," he explained, "believe there's a progression of the soul after death, based on the karma you've accumulated by good deeds and bad behavior and so forth. After death, you get reincarnated already knowing lots of important stuff about life."

"What stuff?"

"Details vary person to person. Reincarnation makes a lot of sense to me. You know how some people seem so much older, even if they're just kids? Like they've already learned from their screwups in another lifetime and don't keep making a stinking mess. Hindus call them old souls. Grown-ups love them because they don't get drunk and go jumping off cliffs or need a lot of lectures about the importance of good dental hygiene. Old souls also have excellent grammar."

I noticed how Milo's voice had gradually lost its sharp, scary edge. It's weird, but the nuts and bolts of dying made him sound really lively and happy, like he was finally getting a chance to share information that he had been carrying around for a long time— Information About Everything That Really Matters to Him in Life.

And of course, Milo wasn't the only person on the transplant unit feeling lively and happy. I felt so much good energy in the room, I let myself be swept away by his stories, the way a good fantasy book has the power to take me out of myself, to shut off the part of my brain that's always worrying or complaining about something. Under the spell of Milo's dreamy voice, I let myself believe, in turn, wholeheartedly in each fascinating description of death.

There was the revenge of pissed-off gods and blinding white lights and sacred three-headed dogs guarding hell and dangerous journeys and great-great-aunts carting the welcome wagon and devils with pitchforks and ghosts who take up housekeeping and a god who tallies up good and bad behaviors like a spiritual accountant.

After a while, I lost track of exactly what Milo was saying. Or even if the stories made sense and how much they contradicted each other. All I knew was that every word out of his mouth was a little spooky and very, very breathtaking.

Milo must have noticed that I hadn't said anything in a while because he stopped right in the middle of describing how Egyptians made mummies ("First, they removed the brain either through the nose or from behind the eye") in order to ask if he was scaring me. Or boring me. Or giving me the creeps. That added to my respect for him. Not only was Milo smart, he was sensitive to others. If he wasn't an old soul, he must be at least middle-aged.

"I do have a question."

"Shoot."

"After all this studying about what other people think, does it help?"

"What do you mean, help?"

"Like . . . like, when—you know—you really think about it."

"Go on," he said.

"Like when you wake in the middle of the night. Like when you wake in the middle of the night and it really hits you where you are. In the hospital and all, and . . ."

"And . . ."

"And you can't explain what woke you, because there was no loud noise or bad dream or pain. But something woke you and you feel it, something creepy. Something creepy creeping."

"Go on," he said again.

"You don't have a name for it, but it's something you recognize. Because it's always there. In the middle of the day when the lights are on and your mom is visiting, you can almost pretend that it isn't there. But at night, it's . . . it's like . . . you know. . . ."

Maybe he didn't know. Maybe he didn't have a clue.

I wanted to take back everything I just said and turn the conversation in a totally different direction. How did I wind up talking like this? This wasn't normal. This wasn't supposed to be part of a boy-girl phone conversation. What was the matter with me?

Why didn't Milo say something?

I lowered my eyes in embarrassment, as if Milo had superpowers and could see me through the wall. My gaze landed on my right arm at the series of tiny bumps where nurses had poked me with needles, sometimes to take blood out, sometimes to put blood in. With the pad of my thumb, I traced the tiny row of raised dots all the way to the inside of my elbow. In some strange way, it was like I could read those bumps the way a blind person reads Braille. What they told me was this: *Say it. Just go ahead and say it.*

Say it because it's real and true and it's what you're

thinking in your deepest thoughts and what you've never said to anyone before. Say it because, if you don't, the opportunity could disappear forever. The moment might just zip off into a black hole and you'll never get a chance to say it to someone else who maybe, just maybe, will understand.

"Dani?"

I took a breath and knew how a dead Egyptian must feel quivering before a lake of fire. I dove in.

"This creeping feeling. At first, you tell yourself that it's going away soon. The doctor will sew in a brand new body part and make everything perfect. And that feels really good for a while, like glitter and sparkles are landing everywhere around you. But then the hair on the back of your neck starts tingling again because you can picture everyone—healthy people, your mom, people who everybody worships like Dr. Alexander, little kids who wear *princess* T-shirts, bus drivers, teachers, yourself. Especially yourself, even if you do get the transplant. It's going to happen eventually. A death sentence. That's what life is. You know it. Not *know* it in the way you know the words to a song, but deeper than that. You know it like it's written with permanent marker on every cell of your body. And knowing it makes you feel so panicked and lonely and sad and scared and confused, because how do you live your life knowing that? So you start to cry, and soon you're crying so hard that you're sure tears are running out of your fingers and toes."

I ran out of air then but managed to get out another sentence. "*That* . . . does your notebook of death help with *that*?"

He took a quick inhale of breath for both of us. "No. I can't say that it does."

TWELVE

I SAW THIS TV show where a really popular girl went to school one morning, and it was as if she had turned into a cockroach. Not a real cockroach like in the famous story by Kafka, which is a really good story, especially since the main character doesn't wake up and discover that it was all a terrible dream. I hate that. Normal, awake life offers plenty of extreme experiences without having to depend on a cheesy it-was-all-a-dream ending.

So in the TV show, someone was spreading rumors that the girl was a disgusting slut-bag, which got everyone whispering about her. Eventually, she became a kinder, gossip-free individual because she had to walk a mile in a slut-bag's moccasins. I didn't get to see the actual ending because my medication was all screwed up and I fell asleep—clunk—about every ten minutes.

But the next day in the hospital, I was feeling a lot like that girl because of all the whispering. It wasn't my imagination. An unusually enormous number of doctors and nurses stopped by to examine me. They spent lots of time conferencing with each other and my mom just outside my door. At first I thought that maybe they had picked up on the romantic tension pulsating between rooms 1 and 2. As I considered it, though, I really couldn't imagine the staff of Children's Hospital gossiping about my love life. Plus, at the hint of anything to do with romance, Mom would definitely be in my face with one of her intimate, girl-to-girl conversations about vaginas, hormones, and methods of contraception. She didn't want me making the same mistake she did, which was to be wild and pregnant at age sixteen.

As if there was any possibility of that.

So it wasn't gossip, but something definitely was going on. There were enough words being expended about me to blow up a tire. When I asked, "What's happening?" Nurse Brianna said that she couldn't officially say anything yet.

Pause.

"I definitely shouldn't say anything." Pause again. She shifted her eyes toward the door, then snapped them back to me. The coast was clear. "I'll get in big, big trouble if the doctors hear that I've revealed even *this* much."

"Cross my wrong-sided heart," I promised.

"You aren't a baby. You have eyes and ears. It isn't fair to keep you totally in the dark. This is your life they're talking about. So, I'll say this one thing: Things may be looking up for you."

"Honest?"

With her index finger, she made the sign of an *X* across her heart.

They forgot to bring us breakfast. That was okay because I'm not a big fan of Cream of Wheat. Then they also forgot to bring lunch, which was really strange. How could they forget with Wendy yelling that she was starved and she wanted chocolate cake right now?

Earlier that morning, Mom had gone home to shower. She was back now, her hair washed and drying in graceful curves over one eye. She kissed me on the forehead, dragged a chair over to my bed, and pulled out her knitting. This was her newest venture for supplementing what she called her "pathetic income." It involved buying scads of cheap yarn, whipping out scarves, and then selling them online as *Glamo Wraps— One-of-a-kind, handcrafted wearable art.*

Mom held up a two-foot length of purple fuzzy stuff interwoven with some gold thread. "On the glamour scale, what do you think? Be honest."

Personally, I thought this particular color scheme

was putrifyingly vile, but I wanted to be encouraging. "Looks good to me. No holes so far."

My stomach growled. I'm sure she heard it, but she didn't say anything. "Mom, can you find out about lunch? I haven't had anything to eat since I woke up. Do you have any sucking candy in your purse?"

She held up a wait-a-sec finger, since she hadn't yet gotten the hang of knitting and talking at the same time. When she got to the end of the row, she didn't go rummaging in her purse for the tasty breath mints that she always kept stocked. Rather she said, "Dr. Alexander doesn't want you to have anything in your stomach because you might be having a procedure today."

Procedure. The very word set my teeth on edge. Mom knew that. Medical people use it to describe everything from drawing a vial of blood to a ten-hour surgery. I heard of one *procedure* where they remove selected organs through your vagina! So why don't they come out and call a blood test a blood test or an operation to remove organs through your vagina an operation to remove organs through your vagina? They should say what they mean.

"What kind of procedure, Beth?" I asked.

"A procedure for which they need you to have an empty stomach. I'm not at liberty to give any more details."

"Not at liberty? Beth! This isn't your X-ray-technician class! You're not my medical professional. You're my mom!"

I thought *that* would get her to spill the secret. Usually she can't keep anything from me. We've been through too much together, all my heart disasters and all her heart disappointments. But she picked up her knitting and started another row. "Sorry, kiddo. My lips are sealed."

The nurse asked if I was up for a visit with Milo.

Of course I wanted to see him. But before I said yes and possibly made a fool of myself, I needed to know if Milo had personally asked to come for a visit or if she had suggested it. "And if that's the case, do you think Milo actually wants to come, or is he only willing to do it as some kind of pathetic mission of mercy, like the senior citizens who come to the hospital once a week and read to us poor, depressed kids?"

Brianna laughed and said, "Oh, this is so sweetly nuts. He asked the same thing about you," before disappearing out the door.

I closed my eyes and tried to imagine what I was going to see when I opened them.

I would see Milo.

Milo coming toward me.

I pictured those sparks in his eyes and other hunky

details like a strong chin and nice white teeth that shined like headlights from across the room.

When I did open my eyes, the nurse was wheeling him in, and he was all that I imagined, in potential at least. In potential, he was probably the most incredible human male alive today on the planet earth. In reality, his bilirubin count must have been way off, because he glowed even more orange than at our first meeting. I also recognized the under-eye dark circles of anemia when I saw them.

He picked off imaginary lint from his PJs. I had to fight a desperate urge to reach under my blanket and scratch the itchy spot where the catheter was hooked up to my body. I groped around for something to say, but of course nothing sophisticated or charming came to mind. My stomach rumbled extra loud. So romantic.

"I'm starved," I blurted out. "I'm *so* hungry I could eat a horse, especially if you took off the shoes."

Milo nodded seriously, which made me worry that he was actually imagining me with pointy, bloody teeth. I was relieved when he asked, "But are you so hungry that you could eat the north end of a south-bound skunk?"

I really liked how he could be so serious and grown-up one minute and then go totally kidlike. The conversation took off from there.

"I just had lunch," he said.

"Lucky you. I'm on the zero-calorie diet because I might be having a *procedure* today. They won't say what kind. Everyone's acting mega mysterious. Did you hear anything?"

"Think about it. It's obvious." When I didn't answer, he said, "No guesses? Okay, I'm going to send you the answer by mind telepathy. The Rosicrucians were really into it."

Milo wiggled his fingers in my face, which practically cast a spell over me because of the little masculine tufts of hair at the base of each one. "I've been practicing on my dog at home, but I'm ready to try it on a human. Get comfortable."

Milo explained how he was going to put all his energy into concentrating his focus. He might even break a sweat, which would smell distinctly like garlic. I, on the other hand, should shut my eyes and let my mind relax until it was blank and open, as spacious as a cloudless sky.

I was skeptical, not really being a true believer in tele-anything, except of course telephones and television. But out of respect to Milo, I kept my eyes closed, except for peeking out four or five times to make sure that he wasn't laughing at me. I would be mortified down to my toes if he was poking fun at my trusting nature. As far as I could tell, though, he was being nondeceptive. His face, with a sharp wrinkle between his eyebrows, was a mask of seriousness. Brilliant but chronically ill people can become a little unstable now and then.

After several minutes, he asked, "Receiving any messages?"

"Not yet. Wait! Maybe. Maybe I smell something."

"Garlic?"

"Yes. A little."

"Really?" He sounded flabbergasted. "You do?"

In all honesty, the garlic was nonexistent, but I didn't want Milo to stop trying. It was thrilling to imagine him entering my mind with his thoughts. Also in all honesty, I didn't really need mind-to-mind communication to get the message. I had already figured out what the nurses and doctors had been whispering about, what Mom wouldn't tell me.

It was what I hoped for and at the same time dreaded because I didn't know what it would mean, how it would change things. Maybe I didn't want things to change.

"A heart," I said, and opened my eyes just as Milo opened his, which caused a butterfly flutter in my chest.

He smiled meaningfully, and I smiled meaningfully back, and that would have been the most perfect moment of my whole life so far—if I had managed to let that moment be and not say another word. Maybe it's because once you start being open with someone, once you've let them peek through the keyhole of who

you are—the crazy middle-of-the-night thoughts—
you can't just stop. At least, I couldn't stop.

It came out in one exhale, thought upon thought,
fear upon fear, layered on each other. How all my life I
wanted to be like everyone else. How getting a new
heart was supposed to be my biggest dream. Only now
that it might become reality . . .

"Maybe it isn't such a good idea. Maybe I shouldn't
be getting it. This probably isn't the right one for me
anyway. Maybe my old heart is the one I'm supposed
to have and I should stick with it. What if I tell Dr.
Alexander that? I want to keep my old heart. Yes!
That's what I want. They can give this new one to
someone else. What if I tell them that?"

"That would be fucked. Fucked and foolish. I col-
lect stories like that."

"Like what?"

"Fucked and foolish ways that people could die."

"Who says I would die? There might be a miracle.
Miracles happen. And what's so bad about being dead
anyway?"

"Yeah, what's so bad about not eating and not
thinking and not talking?" He actually snorted through
his nose. "Here's one of the most fucked and foolish
stories in my collection. Want to hear it?"

I nodded.

"Let's say you have a date with someone you like,
and you really get into the kissing."

"Tongue and all?" I can't believe I blurted that out. But Milo didn't hesitate, just went on with the story.

"Tongue and all. Only he had eaten a peanut-butter cracker and a few crumbs were still in his mouth. He doesn't know that you're allergic to peanuts because you didn't tell him. You thought it would make you seem kind of lame. So while you're kissing, you go into allergic shock. What's the name of that kind of shock?"

I said, "Anaphylactic," and he said, "Yeah, that. And you die. You die from a kiss."

"That would really suck. That's the worst. I can't think of anything more—"

"Fucked or foolish. I have one that's worse. Wanna hear it?"

"Sure."

"It takes a while."

I made a show of settling back into my pillows.

"Okay. It starts with some poor guy with two little kids who dies in a car wreck, and his wife, in the middle of the worst grief you can imagine, decides to donate his liver. Everyone feels good about that, because even though a father is dead, someone else gets to live. Someone is reborn in a way. Only one day, the person with the new liver decides that he's bored of doing all the stuff he needs to do—like taking a dozen pills every day and living a clean, sensible life. He just wants to be, you know, a normal, wild, selfish teenager."

"Milo, I have a question. This teenager—"

"No questions! For a long time, this teenager did everything right. A good, proper patient. He ate right and slept right and drank water and took all his pills and went to all his doctor appointments. Only after a while, he wanted to *not* do everything so right. His friends kept telling him how great drinking is and how you forget all your problems. That's why God invented fermentation. So he decided that more than anything, he wanted to have that teenage experience. He wanted to stop taking his pills. He wanted to drink and drink until he got so happy and shit-faced that he forgot everything, especially how he was different from everyone else."

"So that's what he did?"

"You bet. He spent so much time staring at death, he wanted to make the most out of his life. He lied to his parents and doctors. He ignored all his symptoms. Until one day, the liver from that poor dead dad shut down from all the abuse. His whole body went into rejection, and now it looks like he's going to die. He's going to die 'cause he didn't *feel* like taking a few pills and 'cause he wanted to get drunk. Which, when it comes down to it, isn't two percent as much fun as it's cracked up to be. So, how's *that* for fucked and foolish?"

I didn't know what to say. I wondered, What did he

look like *before*, when he was wild and drunk and selfish? I crossed my arms against my chest and was squeezing myself tight. That was probably to keep me from reaching over and hugging Milo so hard that he would have to peel my arms from around his neck.

I tried to mentally transmit that hug to him, but he didn't seem to get it. He kept staring down at his own clasped hands.

THIRTEEN

THE LATEST CALL FOR Gus Sanchez's services came when he was picking up his son Miguel from morning soccer practice. Gus had just buckled the boy into his seat when his cell phone rang. It was the dispatcher at MTS—Medical Transport Services. "What's up? Delivery?" Gus asked.

"Package will be ready in about an hour. Pick up at Dominican, deliver to Children's Hospital. Not worth using the helicopter. You can make the run just as fast, faster probably."

Dominican to Children's Hospital was ten miles at the most, but there was no way to anticipate a stalled truck or a three-car pileup on the freeway. In a crunch, Gus could improvise along the city streets, saving five minutes here and there, the difference between a live organ and one that would be tossed aside as useless.

"I can make the run in a half hour tops. I'll call when I make the pickup and give you an ETA."

When Gus dropped Miguel at home, the boy pushed his father in the small of his back. "Go, Daddy. Hurry. Drive the heart."

Dr. Alexander came into my room all smiles. "We just got the call. The heart's a good one."

Mom squeezed my hand. Dr. Alexander listened to my chest. The nurse attached a new bag of liquid to my IV pole. "Here's your happy juice. It will make you drowsy, maybe a little loopy." She opened my hospital gown. As if my chest was her canvas, she painted it yellow orange with antiseptic, the color of a summer sunset.

Mom and I waited.

We talked about all the things people would be doing while I was getting my new heart.

"Some people will be doing their job," she said.

"Some people will be taking math tests."

"Watching TV and being bored out of their minds."

I said, "I wonder if anyone will think, *Gee, I wonder who got a new heart while I was having sex.*"

"Dani!"

"What? I *do* wonder that."

"Dani!"

We kept on like this to keep us suspended in the world of medical miracles, where everything was going to lead to my eyes opening, to me going home, back to school and a normal life. We didn't want to talk about all the things that might still go wrong. The infections that could set in. The heart that might be too big or too small. The heart that was perfect in every single way, except that once in my chest, it wouldn't start ticking. No one could predict that. The doctors wouldn't know why, but it just wouldn't start. Things like that happened. And then there was nothing more that anyone could do.

I shuddered. Mom covered me with an extra blanket. Then she leaned over and put her hands on both my cheeks like my whole face was in parentheses.

Gus pulled up in front of Dominican Hospital, where a transplant coordinator waited for him. While exchanging pleasantries about the weather, she placed a red cooler in the back seat and snapped the belt into place. He was surprised when she showed him a second cooler, this one blue. "The heart," she said, and buckled it into the adjoining seat.

Gus signed his name on the form next to the words *Received One Heart, One Kidney.*

A druggy dreaminess settled over me. My eyelids shut, flickered open, shut again.

1, 2, 3, 4, 5, 6, 7, 8, 9, 10, 11, 12, 13, 14, 15.

The number of years alive of my toes, my chin, my elbows, my eyelids. My heart was the first part of me to start forming. I was minus thirty-one weeks old when my heart first came alive. Its beat echoed the rhythm of Mom's own heart.

First, it had been a tubelike thing, but it grew so fast that it needed more space. I pictured it bending and twisting back, forming the familiar shape of chocolate candy boxes.

When a human heart develops, it goes through stages where it resembles the hearts of other animals. The single-chambered heart of a fish. The two chambers of a frog heart. The three chambers of a snake or turtle. The four chambers of a human.

As Gus drove, he wondered about his backseat passengers, not their shape, color, and texture, but where they were going. Into whose life? Into what future? As usual, he had been given only the most basic details—the type of organ and the address.

That felt frustrating, like he was being denied some crucial truth.

Another game to pass the time. We created a Frankenstein-type monster from people we knew. Mom started: "The mouth of my boss, who speaks out of both sides of it."

"The lungs of Wendy," I offered weakly.

"The heart of my boss. His cold, black heart."

I managed to move my lips. "Beth, Mom, you're obsessed. You should get another job."

"You're right."

She checked her watch. Her eyes flickered to the clock on the wall, as if that would tell her something different. "Maybe I should go ask at the nurses' station. Maybe they've heard something more. Nurses are always the first to get the news."

Gus pulled up to Children's Hospital, where a nurse took away the coolers and signed her name—Brianna V.—next to *Received One Heart, One Kidney*. She patted the side of the red cooler and said, "Wendy." Then she held up the blue one and said, "Big thanks from Dani."

"Danny? Little boy?" Gus asked.

"Girl. Fifteen."

"How's she holding up?"

The nurse laughed. "That Dani will be giving this heart a good workout. She's been flirting up a storm with Milo, the boy in the next room. He's waiting for a liver."

They wheeled me down the hallway, into the elevator, and down another hallway to the operating room. Nurses passing by wished me luck. An orderly wheeled me in. Mom didn't let go of my hand.

Maybe it was the drugs, but I started seeing all the things in my life I had lost. At age three, I dropped my favorite stuffed animal, Leon, out of the stroller and went nuts and thought I couldn't live without him. But I could. I did.

Lost books, a scarf, my temper, weight, a parakeet, weeks of school, a best friend, a normal childhood.

All these things, I learned it's possible to live without.

But now maybe I was on the cusp of losing everything.

The anesthesiologist told me to count backward from one hundred. There was music, some kind of opera, and the firm tips of Mom's fingers keeping time with my count: 100, 99, 98 . . .

A pattern appeared before me, swirls of color like a giant lollipop you get at the boardwalk . . . 97, 96, 95 . . . I spiraled down.

When Gus got home, he took his family out for pizza and told them about his workday. He said that he bet Dani liked pizza, too. What teenager doesn't?

His wife wondered aloud if maybe Dani and the boy next door would fall in love for real.

"Mushy." Miguel made a gagging sound and mimed sticking his finger down his throat. He imagined Milo looking exactly like the assistant soccer coach, who said that if Miguel kept his focus, he definitely had the stuff to play high school varsity one day.

All three decided that Dani, Wendy, and Milo were great kids who—with help from Gus—would go on to live long, healthy lives.

FOURTEEN

THE SCHECTERS HAD NEVER been a religious family. They were Jewish, but they didn't keep kosher or even go to synagogue, except when one of their cousins had a bar mitzvah or once a year on Yom Kippur, when they were supposed to be fasting but never actually did.

When it came down to it, Tyler didn't have a clue how his parents felt about their religion or about the questions that plagued him. Did they believe in life after death? Heaven and hell? An immortal soul? Sometimes when his father talked about work, he would say something like, "That house on Woodrow Street is finally going to sell this week, God willing." Or his mother, rolling her eyes skyward and clasping her hands together in prayer, said, "I have only two ADHD kids in class this year. Someone must be looking out for me."

Hearing stuff like that drove Tyler crazy. It made him want to scream in their faces, *Do you really believe that your prayers influence class schedules? Do you think God gives a fuck about your real estate deals? What about war and cancer and little kids burning up in fires? And now Amanda? How about her? How can anyone worship a God who allowed that to happen?*

God.

If there even was a God. The big *if.*

And if there was no God, what was the purpose of anything then—school and friends and family and work and caring and trying—when everyone and everything was just a pathetic fleck of cosmic dust all alone and pointless in the universe?

Did this kind of thinking make Tyler an atheist? Maybe he was.

So it pissed him off that after Amanda died, seemingly the *minute* Amanda died, his parents turned full-tilt Jewish, up to their eyeballs in rituals nobody explained or probably even understood. Plus, they insisted on dragging Tyler, yarmulke on his head, along with them.

Amanda wouldn't be cremated because that went against Jewish tradition. Her body would be washed from head to foot and then she would be buried quickly because *that* was Jewish tradition. At the funeral itself, no one wore dress shoes because Jews in mourning don't wear leather. What was *that* about? And his mother didn't wear perfume, and his father didn't shave.

At the cemetery, the funeral service was as blurry as the unfamiliar Hebrew prayers. All three of them wore strips of black fabric pinned to their shirts to symbolize their loss. Tyler sat in the front row between his parents, his mother's right hand holding his, his father's left arm draped around his shoulders, heavy as a tree branch. More blur, more feelings of being totally disconnected. At his mother's prompting, Tyler tossed a handful of dirt into the grave. He turned away quickly before he could see the clump explode on the lid of the coffin. There was lots of crying and hugging. A couple of old men wrapped in prayer shawls rocked forward and backward like they were on a boat.

And after all that, Tyler didn't get to go home and lock himself in his room. He had to deal with this *sitting shivah* thing. For three days, dozens of people would be filing in and out of their house, offering food, prayers, and condolences. Per tradition, all the mirrors in the house were covered. There was a poster by the front door filled with photos of Amanda under the handwritten words IN HONOR OF HER LIFE.

Ever since returning from the cemetery—it was hours now—his mother had been sitting on a stool in the middle of the living room. Another Jewish tradition.

Her eyes were strangely bright and darting, too alert. Aunt Jen and other women relatives hovered around her, handing her tissues and trying to get her to eat something.

"Claire, just a little taste of this corned beef."

"Claire, you need to keep your strength up."

Tyler's father and his Mom-Mom Florence, his mother's mother, sat on the couch together, holding hands like they were dating. That went beyond weird. Those two hadn't talked to each other in years, not since the divorce, when everyone was forced to take one side or the other. From an end table, Tyler grabbed a glass of wine that someone had left half full. He finished it off in two gulps.

Every annoying relative, every nosy neighbor, every mother who had ever carpooled with the Schecter kids made an appearance that afternoon, and they each eventually homed in on Tyler. Their neighbor Mr. McCoy, whose flower beds Tyler once destroyed by biking through them, put his hands on each of the boy's shoulders and said, "I will so miss your sister. A lovely girl."

When his fourth-grade teacher, the dreaded Mrs. Sugihara, showed up with a box of store-bought cookies, Tyler tried to duck away. She was too quick for him. She took his hand, leaned in, and said in a sticky, sincere voice, "God works in mysterious ways, Tyler."

One of the little gymnasts—Tyler immediately

recognized the sway-backed posture—was pushed toward him by a guy in his twenties with ridiculously broad shoulders, Amanda's coach, Dave. "I'm, you know, sorry about your, um, Amanda," he said, and the little girl added, "She taught me to do a front walkover."

Tyler muttered a cross between "oh, yeah?" and "thanks" and walked away. On a windowsill, he noticed an abandoned glass. Ignoring the red lipstick stain, he swallowed an inch of something sharp and alcoholic.

His great-aunt Minnie, who always smelled vaguely of cooked celery, was next to corner him by the sweets table. When she placed her cold palm flat on his cheek, he felt the hard boniness of the skeleton that lay just below the surface of her wrinkled flesh.

Slightly drunk now, Tyler held up his own hand, which was backlit by the sunlight coming in through the window. An outline of bones, tendons, not much more. He imagined his own skeleton, white as a dried-out seashell. And next to it, he saw his organs like chunks of meat on a sheet of butcher paper at the market. It was a horrible vision.

He stumbled away from his great-aunt, not caring one iota if she thought he was rude. Of course he was rude; he was Tyler. He pushed through the crowded living room, bumped into people without apology, causing some of them to spill drinks. Passing through the kitchen, he grabbed a bottle of wine that had been left open on the counter and kept moving. He wasn't even sure where he was headed until he got there. In a far corner of the house, he entered the sanctuary of the guest bedroom and shut the door behind him.

Alone, quiet.

This was where his mother normally stored junk waiting to go to Goodwill—old sports equipment, obsolete computer components, outgrown clothing in bags. The room was now storage central for the shivah. Every surface held stacks of paper plates, unopened bags of chips, and company serving china.

Tyler shook his head the way a wet dog shakes off drops of water, trying to rid himself of images of skeletons and organs. Tilting back the bottle of wine, he chugged a mouthful and gargled loudly before letting the liquid slide down his throat. It was the Jewish stuff, Manischewitz, thick and sweet like alcoholic Kool-Aid. He took another drink. His forehead and chest expanded with warmth. As he dropped backward onto the bed, a slant of sunlight settled on his face. All that brightness hurt. He twisted around and tugged on the cord of the blinds, turning the room a flat, dim gray. That was better.

"Shivah. Sitting shivah."

He said the words aloud, exaggerating the annoying tone of piety that he'd heard from the adults. The phrase was something that a group of really drunk friends would dare each other to say ten times fast. He took the challenge and amused himself by repeating "Sitting shivah. Sitting shivah." The words had just deteriorated into "shitting sivah" when he heard an appreciative laugh erupt from the other side of the room.

Tyler bolted upright, a puppet whose strings had been pulled taut. "What the . . . ?" He blinked hard in the direction of the laugh, trying to see through the dimness of the room and the thickness in his head. In the corner on the floor sat a man in jeans and button-down shirt, his back against the wall, his arms wrapped around his bent knees. Had he been there all this time? How had Tyler missed him?

"What are you thinking?" the man asked. "That I came in through the bathroom window?" He sang that last part, Beatles-style.

In a clumsy move, Tyler knocked the bottle of wine to the floor. The last few mouthfuls drained out. The carpet sucked it up. Even in the dim light, he could see the big, purple blotch. His mother, the antidrinking cleaning maniac, was going to have a shit fit.

"Seltzer water," the man said.

"Huh?"

"The bubbles in the seltzer are supposed to lift the stain right out."

"Does that really work?"

"You'll have to tell me. Don't wait too long to blot it or it'll set."

Tyler's eyes landed on a tower of paper napkins sitting on a dresser. As he pushed himself to standing, the full force of the alcohol hit. Walking slowly and holding on to furniture, he picked up the napkins and got a better look at the man. Definitely not a teenager or even in his twenties, but nowhere near as old as his parents. Green eyes with heavy lids. A V-shaped point in the middle of the hairline above the forehead. V for vampire. Everything about the man seemed vaguely familiar, as if Tyler knew each of his features individually, but when they were all put together, he turned into a stranger.

"Who are you anyway? A relative, I bet."

"What makes you think that?"

"You have the Schecter lips. Or maybe you're the other side of the family. Your eyes are like my mom's."

"And Amanda's. She had the green eyes, too, right?"

At the mention of his sister, Tyler groped his way back across the room. He placed a thick pile of napkins on the stain and watched the purple design rise to the surface like invisible writing from a magic trick. "Aren't you going to tell me how sorry you are about my sister? How everyone misses her?"

"It takes a lot of courage," the man said.

"For what?"

"It takes a lot of courage to love something that death can touch. That death has already touched."

"What's that supposed to mean?"

"It's something I heard somewhere. Maybe in a history book. Doesn't it sound like something written on a gravestone?"

"What are you, a history teacher? I hate history. So boring."

"Not a teacher. School and I never really got along. I'm more of a history buff. I enjoy hanging out with the already dead."

Tyler had never thought of history like that. *Hanging out with the already dead.* Who was this guy? Nobody in his same gene pool had ever talked to him like this.

Unless.

"Hold on! I know who you are. You're that relative, the cousin. My grandma's sister's daughter's son, or something like that."

The man shrugged. The name came to him. "Aaron, right? The one who isn't married and doesn't have a real job and keeps jumping from one interest to another and won't settle anywhere. The weirdo. Um, no offense."

"No offense taken."

"When your name comes up, they do that clicking tsk-tsk thing with their tongues. You get even more head-shaking than I do."

To demonstrate the relatives' disapproval, the man pursed his lips and gave a quick, tense shake of his head. This was so hilariously accurate that Tyler laughed in big, sucking gulps.

Not a good move. The air went down the wrong pipe and set off a coughing spasm. Some wine moved back up his esophagus and into his mouth. Reflexively, he swallowed it again, syrupy alcohol mixed with stomach acid. Disgusting. It burned hard going back down.

Everything hurt Tyler now, and he groaned. His eyeballs felt lost in his skull, as if they decided to part ways and search for help in opposite directions.

"Manischewitz is a recipe for disaster," the man said. "In future debauchery, stick with vodka. And remember what I said. What did I say?"

Tyler dropped backward on the bed, his head landing on a pillow. "Stick with vodka!"

"Not that. What I said before."

"Before when?"

"Before. Remember?"

Tyler looked at the ceiling. He closed his eyes when it started to spin.

Remember?

About what?

About what?

He never heard the answer.

FIFTEEN

SECOND DAY OF MOURNING, and then the third day. People coming and going, tears and hugs and deli platters. Tyler held on to one thing. As soon as the shivah ended, life would start getting back to normal. It would have to. He wasn't sure what normal would look like anymore, but it wouldn't be this. His mother would have to return to work sometime. His father would stop sleeping in the guest bedroom and go back to his own apartment; he and Tyler would return to their usual divorced-father-son routine, dinner and a movie on the weekends.

But even after the official mourning period was over, life was anything but normal. His father was still there every morning and spending seemingly every waking minute by his mother's side. His parents weren't even fighting. Plus, his mom told Tyler that he could stay home from school as long as he needed. Definitely not normal. She was a freak about his not missing school. He wondered what he could get away with. Three more days, three weeks, three months?

He spent this time holed up in his room playing his entire supply of video games with a goal in mind: twenty-four hours straight. The only breaks he allowed were short naps and trips to the bathroom and to raid the refrigerator for shivah leftovers. The first eight hours of play breezed by. At eleven hours, there was a slump, but a second wind kicked in. Tyler felt it as a new jolt of power being turned on in his brain. Even the dull ache in his wrist from working the buttons and levers disappeared. Electrified, he easily knocked off a particularly tough level ten and settled into that zone of intense concentration where ordinary time and place disappeared and body and mind connected in clear purpose.

Anything felt possible then, everything was under his control. No need to sleep. No need to eat. No sun rising or setting. No worries. No doubt. No fear. No must-dos or should-dos. No world outside of his room. No world outside of his mind. No mind.

No parents.

No dead sister.

No . . .

On the screen, nothing happened. "Come on!" He

clicked, clicked again, but the hero on the screen remained frozen with his hand on a machine gun, an ominous figure in black, poised to pounce. He shut down the laptop, rebooted, but when he restarted the game, it immediately froze at the credits. The next time he tried, a dark screen. He checked the power cord. No problem there. With his right fist, he pounded the cover of the laptop.

It crossed Tyler's mind that he should ask his parents' permission to use Amanda's computer. But he immediately envisioned the whole landscape of repercussions for this simple question: the pained looks, maybe even tears from his mom, all the emotional probing about how Tyler would feel using it and how they felt and what it all meant.

Of course he shouldn't ask permission! He wanted a computer now. No one was using that laptop. Why shouldn't he walk into her room and take it?

For the next few hours, Tyler killed Nazis, completed missions for Mafia dons, and blew up imaginary cities until he was tackling his highest level ever in a particular game. It was outrageously hard. No matter what tactic he used, his character faced annihilation. Then he remembered that he once used his sister's computer, *this* computer, to download a bunch of game-playing tips.

But where had he stored the file? He typed the words *computer games* into the universal search. Nothing. *Tyler*. There it was: *Tyler's stuff.* But before he could open the file, the screen filled with a list of other documents:

Tyler gift ideas.doc

Tyler pix.jpg

He clicked on *The Real complete honest truth about Tyler and me.doc,* and the file opened.

He never finished his video game marathon. He moved on to something even harder to get his mind around.

SIXTEEN

The Real complete honest truth about Tyler and me.doc

SUNDAY

AHGGGGGGGGG. I HATE Tyler. He thinks he can come into my room and use my computer and treat me like I'm a moron who doesn't notice. He doesn't even bother turning it off right, and the keys get all sticky because he's such a gross pig. When I complain to Mom, she's sooooo lame. She promises to talk to him about it. *I'll talk to him about it.* Then even if she does, guess what happens. Nothing!!!!!!!!!!!!!! He gets away with everything because he's got "issues." BFD! This is my diary so I can curse all I want! BFD. BFD. Mom lets him get away with everything.

MONDAY

I tried what Mom suggested and talked to him about using my stuff. Again! That did a lot of good. Not! He's such a jerk. Like when I told him he could *maybe* use my stuff sometimes, but *only* if he asks first and asks in a nice way and then puts everything back in the right place. And washes his piggy hands before he touches anything of mine! Of course, he made faces the whole time I talked. He imitates me like I'm a total prissy priss. Like he really knows the real me. Not! He better stay out of my room or else.

TUESDAY

Tyler said I better stay out of *his* room and then he put all these strings and barricades across the doorway so he'll know if I go in. Like I want to go into his stupid room. I'd need a hazmat suit. It's a toxic pit in there. Yuck.

WEDNESDAY

Tyler and I had another really big fight, and now we aren't talking at all. BFD. He can't use my computer! I don't care if he can't do his homework and he flunks all his classes and he flunks out of school and has to take a boring low-paying job in a doughnut shop and then lives a miserable life selling glazed and jelly-filled ones and nothing interesting ever, ever happens to him. Plus, he has no friends his entire life, especially not a sister who's a famous gymnast and an ER room doctor on top of that. That's the pathetic life he deserves.

THURSDAY

I HATE TYLER IN 6 DIFFERENT TYPEFACES

I HATE TYLER IN 6 DIFFERENT TYPEFACES

I HATE TYLER IN 6 DIFFERENT TYPEFACES

I HATE TYLER IN 6 DIFFERENT TYPEFACES

I HATE TYLER IN 6 DIFFERENT TYPEFACES

I HATE TYLER IN 6 DIFFERENT TYPEFACES

FRIDAY

I HATE TYLER IN 7 DIFFERENT TYPEFACES

SATURDAY

Final thought. Nothing new to add about how much I hate Tyler.

SUNDAY

I'll write something new tomorrow.

MONDAY

Final, final thought. Okay, I've been thinking. The name of this diary that NOBODY will ever read isn't **How I Feel about Tyler When I'm Really Mad at Him.** Or **How Tyler Pisses Me Off** or **Why I Sometimes Wish I Were an Only Child.** The title is **The Real Complete Honest Truth About Tyler and Me.** And the real complete honest truth is . . .

Here goes. I wish Tyler liked me. I really, really, really wish he did and I don't understand why he doesn't. I wish it was like when we were little kids and had secrets together and made up games that other people thought were stupid but really cracked us up. Like the time we renamed Pokey, an old plastic Gumby horse, as Bernie the Belly Bumper and tortured Dad by sneaking up and dancing the toy across his gut. I was probably about seven. I tried telling my friend Hannah about it and she didn't even crack a smile. But to Tyler and me, it was hilarious even after we did it about 100,000 times and Dad didn't even think it was funny anymore.

And oh yeah! The Bernie song Tyler made up. It cracked me up!

I wish I didn't have to pretend that it's no BFD that those good times are gone. I wish I didn't have to act like who cares if Tyler doesn't like me and I don't like him either. I wish we were best friends, even though he's basically a jerk, but there's a lot of good stuff about him, too. Anyway, I'm part jerk myself. I wish I could tell him that. I really want my brother to know things about me that nobody else does. Maybe one day he will. Maybe one day, we'll be friends, even best friends. Fingers crossed. I'm gonna make a list of things about myself to tell Tyler so I don't forget anything important and—

Tyler stopped there. He scrolled back and reread the part about the Gumby horse and hummed a tune. He couldn't believe that he remembered the Bernie song. He had trouble remembering what he did with his homework or where he had put his sweatshirt. Of all the stupid stuff to stick in his brain! Tyler sang a verse. The words spilled out of him.

Before closing the document, he skipped to the end and read and reread Amanda's closing line from that Monday night a couple of weeks ago:

There. That's it, the real complete honest truth about Tyler and me straight from my heart.

SEVENTEEN

I OPENED MY EYES. I heard a loud, steady beat in my ears.

Something was wrong, something in my chest, hard and heavy and way too powerful.

A hand closed around my right foot. I flinched slightly from the cold fingers. Mom squeezed my toes tighter. "Dani, your foot. It's so warm. Now I know everything's going to be all right."

I took a deep breath, and it was sweet, cool, and moist. There was so much of it, I gasped. I was drowning in air.

I kept waiting for a clue about whose heart I had.

I waited for a craving for egg rolls or a sudden desire to go on a murderous rampage or a preference for math over English or the memory of someplace I'd never been.

I waited for dreams about somebody I'd never met.

I waited for something, anything. If a cell can remember that it's the cell of a heart or a toenail or a nose, what else could it remember?

While Dr. Alexander examined me, she insisted that I wouldn't be feeling anything like that. "Impossible, Dani. Personality and memories reside in the brain. Now, maybe if you had a brain transplant. But so far that only happens in science fiction."

"I have a lot of energy. I've never had this much energy. Maybe the heart came from someone hyper."

"You lived with your old tired heart for so long you got used to it. This is a big adjustment. You're finally feeling what a teenager with a normal heart feels like. No wonder you're ready to turn cartwheels. It's no big mystery." She poked at the scar that ran down my chest like a zipper, checking for signs of infection.

"Ouch!"

"Sorry. It's healing perfectly, but the incision will be tender for a while."

Dr. Alexander continued on about how individual organs and cells don't carry and transfer memories, likes, or dislikes. And while she was talking, it all made perfect scientific and medical sense, which I had no reason to doubt because Dr. Alexander graduated from a top medical school.

But still. *Still.* It didn't make sense to me in the

human experience way. Consider the kiss. Two people fall head over heels in love when mouth meets mouth. One minute you're strangers. The next, you know each other in the deepest way that two human beings can ever know each other. And that's only a little bit of saliva being swapped. What about a heart?

So I kept waiting for clues, but it was all disappointment. Yes, I had more energy, but I was still me. I didn't have a sudden understanding of advanced physics. When the thought of a hamburger arose, I didn't want mustard instead of my usual ketchup. I had hated country music with all of my old heart. I still hated it with the new one.

Courageous and brave, strong and tough. Everyone had a label for me. After the transplant, I was a living, breathing grammar lesson in superlatives.

Dr. McGarry, leading a group of surgery residents to my bedside: "How's the most plucky, bravest cardiac patient in the world?"

A get-well card from a bunch of eleventh-graders I hardly knew: You Are Our Hero!!!!!

A get-well card from my cousin Cara: To the gutsiest person in our family.

When Nurse Brianna changed my catheter bag, she held it up like it was the severed head of a monster I had slain for the good of the entire universe, instead of a bag full of pee that had leaked out of me. "Keep up the good work, Dani."

Card attached to a stuffed lion from the people who work with Mom: To Dani, who has the spirit and courage of a lion.

All this attention gave me the creeps. It's not that I'm one of those seriously reserved people who doesn't like attention. I very much like attention, but only if it's true and deserved. Hearing the word *brave* applied to me made me feel . . . pardon me while I choke on my tapioca.

Brave is pushing past firefighters and, without a thought for my own safety, rushing into a burning building to rescue a three-legged dog that's cowering under the bed.

Brave is volunteering to go to a country where they don't have the world's most advanced medical devices, such as they had at Children's Hospital, and being kind and helpful to people suffering from a horrible skin-eating bacteria that makes their noses fall off.

Brave is walking up to the meanest girl at school and saying what is truly the truth: "Melissa, the way you feel good about yourself is by making fun of everyone else. Maybe one day karma will catch up and give you a contagious skin-eating bacteria and *then* see how popular you are."

Brave is doing *that*.

It's making a decision to do something that nobody is forcing you to do. You just do it. Because it has to be done. Because it's the right thing to do. Because no one else has the guts to do it.

The truth is, I didn't volunteer to have a transplant. Nobody asked if I would agree to be born with a messed-up heart so that someone else didn't have to suffer. Honestly, if someone *had* asked, I would have said, "Go ahead and put Melissa's heart on the wrong side of her body and give *her* the bargain-basement valves. That's fine with me."

An important thing to know about hospitals: The staff doesn't let you get away with being sick too long. As soon as possible after surgery, nurses get you up and walking, even if you make unladylike groans the entire time.

Another thing: If you're between ages five and eighteen, they insist that facing death is no excuse for remaining uneducated. At Children's Hospital, there was a person whose entire job consisted of making lesson plans for kids who sleep twenty hours a day and can hardly remember their own name. The teacher's name was Mrs. Froid, which just so happens to mean "cold" in French.

A week after the surgery, Mom was helping me back into bed after a walking tour of my hospital room when Mrs. Froid appeared. I didn't notice her at first because she was preceded by Joe the nurse (also not noticed), who was preceded by Milo in a wheelchair. I only had eyes for him.

"Wow. You look great," Milo said.

Joe winked at me. "Slow down, Romeo. She's got a new heart. Let's not give it a full workout right off the bat."

Milo twisted around. "I meant she looks great in the medical sense." Then to me: "You know, pink. You look pink."

"It's okay, Romeo. She does look great."

"Pink!"

"Really?" I asked. "You think I look great? Pink? You look . . ."

"Still orange," Milo filled in.

"Pink or orange, we must keep our minds active," Mrs. Froid said. "The brain is a muscle. It atrophies if not exercised."

She then made a big deal about having Mom and Nurse Joe leave the room because they would be distractions from the *educational process*, which is what she called this visit. I considered it more or less a date. Mrs. Froid was the unwanted chaperone.

"Let's get started." She handed us each a copy of a novel. The cover showed Civil War soldiers at battle with a backdrop of the American flag. *The Red Badge of*

Courage—176 pages. At least it wasn't too long. The bad news: The author had been dead a long time. The book wasn't written in this century. It wasn't even written in the *last* century.

I read the back cover, and certain words jumped out at me: *war, wounds, fear, pain, death.*

Ugh.

Given my personal history with blood and suffering, I definitely would have preferred a romance. Did *The Red Badge of Courage* even have any girl characters? When I leafed through the pages, I noticed lots of underlining, hopefully some essay help from the previous critically ill person forced to read an American classic.

Mrs. Froid clapped her hands for attention, even though there were just two of us who were already perfectly attentive. Milo raised one eyebrow in my direction to make sure I noticed how ridiculous she was. We shared the moment, proving once again that the shortest distance between two people is a joke at someone else's expense. After that, Mrs. Froid went on for a while about the author's life and what was happening in America at the time and the importance of the novel in the Western literary canon and the glory of the language.

"Although the story is deceptively simple, it reveals the full horror of war, while delving deeply into the complexity and unpredictability of human behavior. That's all I'll say today. I don't want to take away from your own reading."

It wouldn't have been Mrs. Froid if she left without giving us an assignment. "Read the first twenty pages. Think about the motivation of the major characters. Pay careful attention to motifs, symbols, and so forth."

"SparkNotes?" I asked with hope.

"No SparkNotes! But you may do your reading together today. Encourage each other."

Then Mrs. Froid left me alone with Milo. This wasn't going to be so intolerable after all. He tossed his *Red Badge* onto my bed. "It's not a bad book."

"You read it before?"

"Yeah, I've been around *The Red Badge of Courage* block two or three times. It's on every reading list ever created. How did you manage to avoid it? Oh, right, you had the organ-shutting-down homework excuse."

"So, what's the story about?"

"This guy. His name is Henry something, but the author always calls him the youth. That's so you don't think the story is only about one person in one place at one particular time. It's more universal."

"Like City Mouse or Catwoman."

"Sort of. Well, yeah, exactly, only this isn't a comic book or folk tale. It's realistic. The youth is a northerner who gets all caught up in the flag-waving and rah-rah of the times. To prove he's a man and a real patriot, he goes against his mother's wishes and enlists in the Union army."

"Very brave."

"That's what he's trying to prove. Only, it's not so simple. He gets all twisted in his head wondering if he really *is* courageous."

"Of course he's courageous! He volunteered."

"But how's he going to act when the bullets start flying? Will he stand and fight, or will he sneak away? Will he be brave, or is he just a macho bullshitter? If you want to impress Froid, tell her that a major theme of the book is that courage takes different faces. People think they're going to be brave, but when—"

"Milo?"

"What?"

"Does the book . . . does it say anything about . . . let's say someone goes through a really terrifying experience, something that most people in the world will never have to experience."

"Like the youth in the Civil War?"

"Sort of. Only this isn't something they volunteered for. They had no choice."

"People always have a choice."

"But the other choice was even worse. So does that count as being brave and courageous?"

Milo thought awhile before answering. "I don't see why not."

"Really?"

"Sure. That kind of bravery happens all the time."

"Like what?"

"Remember the Egyptian death thing that I told you about? Each soul has to battle monsters and boiling lakes, no help from anyone, and whether you want to or not. No one asks for volunteers."

"I guess that does count as courage."

"Or how about this. Let's say you've been out sick from school for weeks and you have to take a test anyway and you just suck it in and do the best you can. Bravery's a state of mind."

I never thought about it like that. Bravery isn't just what you're doing. It's the attitude when you're doing it. I came up with my own example then, something I wanted to talk about, even though Milo might not. I was worried about my timing. I might ruin a perfectly good date by bringing up the wrong topic, which this probably was. Still, my mouth got the better of my romantic good sense.

"Let's say you've already been through one terrifying ordeal, and after you survived it, you make a really dumb mistake. Which, in my opinion, any human being could make, it's nothing to be ashamed about. Only, because of the mistake, you have to go through the same ordeal all over again. Most people don't have to do this even once. You have to do it twice! You don't want to, but you're doing it anyway."

When the space between Milo's brows crinkled, I quickly added, "Wait! I don't mean *you* you. I mean, the universal you. So what do you think?"

He dropped his eyes; his lashes were so long. "This *you* person is still a total idiot. But I guess it counts as bravery, especially if *you* learned something from your mistakes and don't bitch and moan about how unfair life is."

"Like you said, bravery is a state of mind." I could have stopped there, remaining in the universal. That would have been the safe thing to do. But it didn't feel right. "Milo, I think that you, *you* in the personal sense, you are very—"

That was when Milo proved to me just how courageous he actually was. He finished my sentence and added something of his own: "brave. You, too, Dani. I think you are the most brave scared person I ever met."

EIGHTEEN

Dear Big Girl,

Do you like your new heart?
Check one

YES   NO   MAYBE

A poem about my new kidney
Roses are red
Violets are blue
What color are kidneys?
Purple and pink, too
Knock knock who's there?

Kid
Kid who?
Kid knee.
Get it?
lOVE WENDY Write back

Dear Big Girl,
You should write back!!!!!!! Now!!!!!! My
mom's helping me write a letter to the
family of the person who gave me my
new kidneys. She says I have to do it!
It was really nice of them to give me
the kidneys. Here's my letter so far

Every time I pee, I think of you.
Kidneys=pee. THANKS FOR THE
KIDNEYS!!!!!!!!!!!!!!!!!!!!!!!!! Love, Wendy

Things shaped like kidneys

Beans

Swimming Pool (no diving board)

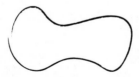

Oil Leak Under Daddy's Car

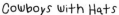

Cowboys with Hats

Do you think I'm a good drawer & letter writer for 8? Check one

YES	NO	MAYBE

Dear Big Girl,
Are you drawing hearts in your letter to your heart family? If you need help, I'm good at it. Here's a bunch of bee-u-ti-ful hearts you can use if you want.

Dear Big Girl,

When you finish your letter and I finish mine, we can put them in the same envelope because—GUESS WHAT??????????—they are going to the same place!!!!!! Did you know that? It means we are sisters. I ASKED BUT my mom says you still can't come live with us. I'll nag her really, really hard. Write back, that's an order!!!!!!!!!!!!!

love, wendy

NINETEEN

IN BOOKS AND MOVIES, love stories always have two sides. The Before (the loneliness, the unnoticed sunsets) and the After (the hand-in-hand walks, the happily ever after). However, even though I personally have not yet experienced the full brunt of romance, I have seen things from Mom's perspective, starting with the wannabe rock star who was my father for about ten minutes and continuing through a whole flowchart of boyfriends. I can talk from that. Love is definitely more complicated.

The same holds true for organ transplants. Unlike the simple, rosy version handed out to the general public, After is not all perfect blood pressure and pink cheeks and going wild at school dances. Cutting a person open and inserting someone else's heart into her chest cavity is not the end of the story. In many ways, it's just the beginning.

Nurse Brianna stood before me with a line of pills of many shapes, sizes, and colors on a shiny silver tray, like a gourmet meal for astronauts. "Okay, Dani, what's the name of this white pill, and how often do you need to take it?"

Nurse Joe chimed in. "And what are the side effects? And what do you do if you notice a side effect?"

Welcome to my post-op medication quiz. I was already a star pupil. For example, I knew that the little amber capsule in the silver foil packet would suppress my immune system. On the surface, that might not seem like a very good idea, given the amount of disgusting germs waiting for the travel opportunity of a sneeze or a French kiss. Most health-conscious people stuff themselves with echinacea to *bolster* their immune system. I, however, needed to take pills to shut mine down. Left to itself, my body would attack the new heart for the stranger that it was.

Unfortunately, though, a suppressed immune system doesn't discriminate very well. Along with not rejecting the heart, my body now didn't reject all sorts of bacteria and viruses. They could blossom into mouth sores and yeast that grows like white, hairy fuzz on my tongue. Lovely and tasty. Therefore, I also needed to take antibiotics (yellow pill, three times a day).

(One bit of good news about a suppressed immune

system: I was forever excused from cleaning the toxic waste in a kitty litter box. Doctor's orders. That might come in handy one day, if Mom ever lets me get a cat.)

All told, there were twenty-two pills in my buffet. Some I took every day, some on a timetable that made a school block schedule seem simple to follow. The white pill was for . . . was for . . .

Like the hosts of a TV game show, the nurses waited for my answer with round, enthusiastic eyes. I looked for help in Mom's direction. She pretended to knit while trying to slip me the answer. She mouthed something that looked like *star* . . . what? *Star oink?*

"No cheating!" Brianna insisted. "You both have to know the drug regimen. It's important." She handed the white pill to me, along with a glass of water. I swallowed.

I got it. Star oink. Steroid.

"Possible medical side effects from steroids," I recited from memory. "Puffy, round face, bone weakening, obesity, stretch marks, increased cholesterol, muscle weakness, and mood swings."

"*Possible* side effects. And they're only temporary," Brianna assured me. "After a while, the doctor will taper down on the pills."

"Before you know it," Mom insisted.

"And let's not forget increased hair growth and acne from the cyclosporine," I added.

I was already starting to see all the dreaded side

effects when I looked in the mirror. I had chipmunk cheeks. Tufts of hair sprouted on my upper lip and chin. Dark, coarse hair was filling in the space between my eyebrows faster than tweezers could eliminate them. Long, masculine hair snaked around my arms and legs. I had hair growing long and thick and black in all the exact places a girl my age doesn't want hair. I could hardly wait for the stretch marks.

> *Dear Donor Family,*
> *How are you?*

> *Dear Donor Family,*
> *Just a note to tell you how much I'm enjoying the heart DUMB, DUMB, DUMB*

> *Dear Donor Family,*
> *I don't know why you'd want a letter from me since I'm alive and someone you love is dead and you don't know me and can't possibly care about me, so what could I say that would mean anything to you? You probably want to take this letter and rip it into a million pieces and then burn the pieces. Go ahead! Be my guest! I totally understand.*

"Mom, should I really write a letter to the family?"
"Only if you want to."

"What should I say?"

"What do you want to say?"

"I don't know. Nothing seems right. What if things were the opposite?"

"Meaning?"

"If I was the one who died? If you gave away my heart?"

Mom's hands tightened around her knitting needles. "Dani, I don't want to go to that scenario right now."

"Come on, Beth! Would you want to get a letter from the person with my heart?"

"Maybe. No. Yes. I guess I would."

"What would you want it to say?"

"Not 'I'm sorry for your loss.' Definitely not that. I would have had my fill of that. So many well-meaning people not knowing what to say, so they all say the same thing."

"Then what, Mom?"

"Nothing clichéd, that's for sure." She finished her row. "I guess I'd just want to know."

"Know what?"

"About you. Who you are. From the beginning."

Dear Donor Family,

To begin at the beginning of me, I was born with a messed-up heart.

My name is Danielle, only everyone calls me Dani.

I just turned fifteen and a half, and I have no body piercings.

I'm in tenth grade.

On my last report card, I got one A, three Bs, and no Cs, Ds, or Fs.

I live in an apartment with my mom.

The color scheme of my bedroom is pink and orange, which isn't as clashy as it sounds.

I wear a size six and a half shoe.

My hair is usually long, only now it's short and unflattering because it's easier to take care of in the hospital.

I'm currently reading The Red Badge of Courage, *an American classic. It's better than I thought, but you can get along just fine in life if you never read it.*

I enjoy talking to interesting people who know about things that I don't, and soon, I hope to travel and have lots of adventures.

I phoned Milo and read the letter to him. "It's only a first draft. What do you think? Honestly."

"It's okay."

"Just okay?"

"It's kind of obitty."

"Huh?"

"Like an obit, obituary. You were born and go to school and live here, et cetera, et cetera."

"Really? An obit? I was trying for a MySpace feel. An obit probably isn't in the best taste."

"Nothing wrong with an obit, as long as it's interesting. No offense or anything, but yours is a snore. I've written plenty of obits."

"For friends who died? I'm sorry."

"No, obits for myself. It's kind of a hobby. Hold on."

Papers rustled. Milo whistling, then back on the line. "Here's the first one I ever wrote. I must have been around eight."

"You still have it?"

"I saved them all. Given my liver situation, I never knew when an obit would come in handy. Ready? *Milo Nutley, billionaire inventor of the Tasty Milo Nut, surfing and spelling champion, mourned by millions.*"

"What's a Milo Nut?"

"No such thing. It's the nickname from hell that started in first grade. I couldn't get rid of it. Plus, I never surfed in my life, and my spelling sucks. God, I was a weird little kid."

"All little kids are weird."

"Here's another. Fifth grade: *Milo Nutley, person of mystery, dead before his time.* What does that even mean? If you're dead, that's your time to be dead, right? How can it be before your time? What was I thinking? Oh, man, listen to this. I forgot about this one: *Milo Nutley, a seventh-grader at Bayside Middle School, died today using his tenth-degree black-belt skills to save the entire school from certain annihilation by a deranged karate expert from Planet Xendo.* See what I mean about obits? They have to be interesting."

"But, Milo, those aren't true."

"They're the product of the deranged mind of a little kid. But that's my point—interesting is more important than true. Who cares if people call you a liar when you're dead?"

"Do you still write them?"

Milo muttered something. I asked, "What?" and he answered, "Yeah, I do. Only not so deranged. They have more truth in them now." I begged him to read his latest one. I was completely obsessed with the idea of learning anything new and true about Milo.

"Come on. You can help me add some spice to my own life story, which, as you said, is terminally boring."

"I did start a new one last night. So far, I only have the last line. *Milo Nutley's final wish is—*" He paused. "I have an idea. Tell you what. Think about it for a while. Then, you tell me your final wish, and I'll tell you mine. Deal?"

> *Dear Donor Family,*
> *Maybe you might be interested in hearing about*
> *my final wishes because, as you might suspect, they*

can tell you a lot about a person. Such as what a person values and hopes to accomplish in life, and whether or not that person is selfishly obsessed only with their own happiness at the expense of everyone else, like most of the girls in a certain high school I'm familiar with.

Or whether the person wishes for things with a higher purpose, such as stopping all wars and curing cancer and making beautiful art and music in the name of world peace and saving the orphaned elephants of the world, of which there are far too many. I'm definitely the kind of person with final wishes of this higher sort.

But to be perfectly frank, I also think that anyone saying they want ONLY world peace, etc., etc., is probably self-delusional or hoping to win Miss Death Bed Congeniality or to get into heaven no questions asked. Well, the pageant judges might be fooled, but heaven won't be. I bet that God (or any Godlike substitute of your choice) understands that it's okay for some final wishes to be unlofty. As my mom always says, "Don't shoot me! I'm only human."

So, my list of final wishes—which I boiled down to ten so you won't be bored out of your mind—includes both the good-for-the-world and the good-for-me kind. The List:

1, 2, 3, and 4. All previously mentioned items—the end of war, cure for cancer, world peace,

art/music, and proper homes for
elephants.

5. A high-paying job with good benefits for my mom
   that allows her to use her creative side and makes
   her stop complaining about her boss all the time.
6. A romance with someone obsessed with me in a
   sexual way that's a little inappropriate for my age.
7. Lots and lots of fatty, good-tasting food.
8. No furry animals being gutted and skinned so rich
   ladies can wear fur coats.
9. Global warming reversed immediately.
10. A new liver for my friend Milo, and not just so he
    can be obsessed with me etc., etc. He really
    deserves a new liver so he can stop feeling bad
    about his last transplant and get on with his life.
   Well, Donor Family, I hope you aren't offended by any
of my wishes and decide that the wrong person got your
loved one's heart and that you want it back immediately. I
don't think there's anything I can do about that.
                    Sincerely yours,
                    Dani

"And finally, number nine: Global warming
reversed immediately," I read into the phone. I chick-
ened out revealing number ten and shortened number
six to: a romance.

"My turn?" Milo asked.

"Your turn."

He cleared his throat. "Milo Nutley's final wish. If he doesn't get a second liver, Milo Nutley hopes that his heart is in good shape. He wishes that it goes to someone who needs it and deserves it, someone who will use every beat of it to live a great, long life."

By the way, I never sent that particular letter to the donor family. I kept my first letter to them short, maybe a little boring according to Milo standards. I thanked them. I told them a little about myself. My last lines were: *I know that your life will never be the same. Neither will mine. My doctor said that there couldn't have been a more perfect heart for me.*

TWENTY

MORE THAN A MONTH had passed since Amanda's death. Her parents were doing as well as could be expected. That's what everyone said. Claire could finally say "Amanda" aloud, without the name lodging in her throat. Robert had moved back into his own apartment, but he still had dinner with his ex-wife and son two or three times a week. That felt weird and tense at first. Gradually, though, they talked more and more about everyday things, like Tyler's upcoming exams or the house that Robert's agency just put on the market for sale. The parents had even taken the first step toward cleaning out Amanda's room. Steeling themselves, they crossed the threshold and gathered up textbooks to return to her school.

So when Helen Curry from the transplant network asked if the family would like to receive letters from the organ recipients, Claire gave a hesitant yes. Up until then, she had known only the most basic details. That's all she could handle. There was a local teenager who got her daughter's heart. Something about a third-grader. Was it the liver or a kidney?

By the time the letters actually arrived, Claire had more or less put them out of her mind. They came on an ordinary Saturday, dropped into the mail slot by the ordinary mailman, the letters bundled in an ordinary tan envelope with an ordinary postal meter stamp and the Transplant Network as the return address. She ripped the envelope open and shook out the contents.

Three sealed white envelopes. *To the Donor Family. To the Donor Family. To the Donor Family.*

Until that moment, Claire had thought she was ready. She wasn't. Her eyes settled on the letters with the growing fury of a housecat looking down from a window onto a trio of neighborhood toms that had made themselves at home in the backyard. This was wrong! They didn't belong here! Claire actually hissed at the envelopes, the exhalation pressing hard against the backs of her teeth.

With a quick sweep of her hand, she stuffed the letters into the big envelope and jammed it into the back of a file cabinet. She slammed the drawer closed with a hard, satisfying clank. All that day and next, Claire couldn't walk through that room without feeling the presence of the letters, like she was slogging through a bog to get away from them.

A few nights later, she dreamed that she was wandering blindly and barefoot through a snowstorm. The flakes were large, white, and square, stinging like paper cuts as they fell on her face, shoulders, and feet.

"Tyler, wake up!"

It was 5:45 A.M.

"Mom, what? What's going on?"

"Lighter fluid. Give it to me. And matches."

"I don't have lighter fluid!"

That was contraband material, family rules. So Tyler denied it fervently, even though he did have a practically full can of Zippo hidden in his bottom dresser drawer under the chaos of dirty socks and underwear. His mom repeated her request. This time, there was something about her tone—calm and impersonal, as if placing an order in a hardware store—that told him it was okay. Tyler went into his hidden stash and followed her down the stairs, through the kitchen, and into the backyard. She didn't offer an explanation, and he didn't ask for any.

Outside, his mom sat cross-legged on the slab of concrete where Amanda had drawn hopscotch grids and Tyler had bounced balls for hours at a time. She patted the space next to her, and he took a seat. The ground felt cold through his sweats. The half moon, a clown's too-wide grin, hung directly overhead.

"I hate these people," she said. Her voice was strangely flat in contrast to the word *hate*.

"What people, Mom?"

"I know they didn't do anything wrong, but I hate them."

It unnerved Tyler to hear his mother talk this way, especially in the dark in that eerie calm and controlled voice. But even more, it thrilled him. This was so unlike her. His mother got along with everyone, and it usually drove Tyler nuts. If he ruled the earth, scores and scores of people—certain teachers and annoying neighbors, stuck-up classmates, neighborhood brats, bad actors, politicians, public figures of all sorts—would be immediately banished to another planet in another dimension. And now, like him, his mother was also full of hate.

He watched as she shook out the contents of a brown envelope and tried to lean three white envelopes against each other in a tepee shape. When they kept collapsing, Tyler took over. Wadding up a piece of old newspaper from the recycle bin, he used it as a base and the tepee stood.

"Not big enough," his mother said. "I want it big. I want it to go on for a while."

Tyler surrounded the letters by a moat of balled-up

newsprint. His mother went into the house and returned with some additions: a dental appointment reminder card for Amanda, her renewal forms for USA Gymnastics, some late-arriving sympathy cards. Tyler added more newspaper, a sheet of cardboard, and some old cellophane wrapping.

"Perfect," his mother said.

"Now?" he asked.

"Now."

He squirted the pile with lighter fluid. The stream made an arc and caught glints of moonlight. He was well aware that his mother wasn't scurrying around all nervous and parentlike to make sure things remained safe. Tyler had never before felt so trusted by her.

"Move back," he ordered, and she did.

With one match, the edge of a piece of newspaper turned orange and then caught fire. There was a crack of cellophane. In another minute, the whole pile ignited. It burned steadily, not too quickly. Tyler liked everything about this fire, about any fire, really—the colors you never see anywhere else, the smells, the tickling on the inside of his nose, the sense of peace followed by the sudden pop that never failed to make him feel very alive.

His mother's cheeks flushed slightly pink from the heat as she watched flecks of ash, like snow in reverse, drift skyward and out of sight.

TWENTY-ONE

TYLER DIDN'T STEAL IT.

In the moonlight, he had noticed that all three letters were addressed to him. *To the Donor Family*. He was family. A brother. It wasn't stealing to take something that practically has your name on it. In his life, he had walked off with stuff that he had far less right to take than this. Money from his mother's handbag, pens from Amanda's room, batteries from Wal-Mart. He hadn't felt guilty about those things. These letters actually belonged to him.

So when his mother wasn't looking, he grabbed one of the envelopes and quickly slipped it into the pocket of his sweats. He felt its solid shape pressing on his thigh as the other two letters burned and turned to ash.

With the first hint of daylight in the sky, Tyler left

his mother sweeping up the backyard and returned to his bedroom. He switched on his desk lamp and ripped open the letter. It had a Florida postmark.

Dear Donor Family,

As you notice, I've written this letter not on a computer, but on my old-fashioned typewriter. I don't even own a computer. That should tell you I'm no spring chicken.

Someone who's reached my advanced age should have the words for almost every situation. But I feel at such a loss for what I want to say to you. How do you thank someone for everything?

The hospital social worker, that dear heart, says that I shouldn't try to be flowery, which is not my nature anyway. There are greeting cards for that kind of sentiment. She says I should tell you my story so that you can see your gift for yourself. So here it is, a bit long-winded but such as it is.

Twenty years ago, when I first moved to the Villages of Boca Raton in Florida, most everyone was around sixty-five years old, and you never saw such a group of spry retirees, just like in the ads, always swimming or playing tennis. My husband, Marty, a former dentist—may he rest in peace—loved nothing more than a good round of golf.

What they don't show in the ads is what they wouldn't dare show because it would send potential residents running in terror. Nobody living here is young for their age anymore. After two decades, we're all falling apart a section at a time, arteries clogging, kidneys shutting down, feet as cold as dead fish. All the little things that used to go away don't anymore. If only we knew then about the importance of calcium, we wouldn't have so many bodies twisted like question marks sitting around the pool.

Once, sometimes twice a week, an ambulance, sirens screaming, comes tearing through the Villages. For me, that sound unleashes questions: Did the poor soul have any inkling her time was up? What did she tell her loved ones about what finally, ultimately, at the end was important in her life?

I'm not by nature a morbid person, and I've never been particularly religious. But I don't think you have to be in order to have these kinds of questions. And I know I'm not alone in having them. When the sirens start, it gets very still. People in the clubhouse stop making their crafts. The swimmers hook their arms on the side of the pool. Even the noisy Florida birds stop their chirping, as if they're considering whether or not they're making good use of their time on this earth.

Up until recently, I've been one of the lucky ones. Knock on wood. But when you turn eighty-four like I just did, you're asking for it. Sometimes late at night, I would wonder, So, Miriam, old gal, what will it be? Breast cancer? Heart attack?

The big problem turned out to be my eyes. Who would have figured? They were once hazel beauties. I had not given them a thought in years, except to note with a certain sadness how wrinkled they'd become, heavy-lidded like a toad's. But then the clouding started. It got worse and worse, until I was looking at the world through wax paper.

What kind of life would I have if I could no longer read, play canasta, look out at the ocean, or see the smile of my first great-grandchild, who's on her way into the world?

One of my eyes couldn't be saved. The doctor hoped that a cornea transplant on the other would give me some sight. I prayed that the doctor was right.

He was.

Many evenings now, I sit on my deck and watch the sky for hours through my good right eye. I'm mesmerized, sometimes moved to tears by its clarity. I swear, there are two hundred different shades of dark. I never realized that before. And the stars!

If my husband the pessimist were still around, he would say something about how the stars are all the terrible questions, desperate pleas to God, longings, fears, and disappointments that had ever been expressed by human beings.

I would drape my arm around him and say, "Marty, you know I'm no Pollyanna. But maybe those stars are all the prayers that have been answered, mine included."

Donor Family, that's what I want to say to you. You are my answered prayer. You are the star that keeps the light shining.

Thank you, thank you, and thank you again.

Yours truly, Miriam P.

TWENTY-TWO

TYLER FLIPPED THE LETTER over hoping for a post-script, some last-minute thought that the woman needed to get down on paper or the insight might be lost forever.

He didn't want the letter to end. There was a sense that as long as the paper remained in his hands, Miriam P. would still be communicating with him, despite the gap of three thousand miles and more than sixty years of age. He pictured her, an old woman looking to the stars.

She had never before been mesmerized—that was *her* word—by the stars and shades of the night sky. Did this passion rise spontaneously as the doctor placed the cornea on her eye like a crystal dome over the face of a watch? What did it mean? Where did it come from? Was there anything, even at the very edges of her vision, that seemed to belong to someone else?

Ever since reading *The Real Complete Honest Truth About Tyler and Me.doc,* he had avoided his sister's laptop. He feared it in the way he had feared the dark as a little kid. Who knew what would jump out of the computer if he switched it on again? What words or sounds or images would appear out of the dark, unsummoned and unwelcomed, with the touch of a key? Only now, Tyler felt compelled to turn it on. He Googled the word *cornea* and read randomly.

The thin, transparent membrane consists of five layers. It bends light.

Despite its seeming lack of substance, the cornea consists of organized proteins and cells.

With no blood vessels to nourish it, the cornea feeds on tears.

The cornea that once fed on his sister's tears now sat on the eye of this woman who stared at the Florida sky every night.

Could one person's vision be transferred to another? Donor's tears to recipient's sight?

Tyler searched his memory and came up with fleeting images that connected his sister to the sky and to the stars—Amanda staring out the window, Amanda lying on her back on the lawn—but nothing conclusive. He searched her documents for the word *star*. The screen filled.

One file contained Amanda's team photo, the Tumbling All-Stars. He clicked it closed. In Staranswers.doc, he found a homework assignment from Amanda's earth science class.

Page 97, answers to 1 & 2.

1. The star nearest to our solar system is the triple star Proxima Centauri, which is trillions of miles from earth.

2. The number of stars visible to the naked eye from earth has been estimated to total 8,000. Some of those stars are a million light-years away.

Only one remaining entry looked promising, a long document labeled *Random Star Thoughts.* References to stars jumped out.

Sometimes when I can't sleep, I like looking out my window, especially when it's a clear night like now. Some of these stars are a million light-years away, which means the light I'm seeing was created when I was negative 999,986 years old. That gives me the chills.

When I look at the night sky, I always hear that deep voice at the beginning of *Star Trek* reruns. "Space, the final frontier. These are the voyages of the Starship *Enterprise*, her five-year mission . . ."

There's a lot to know about space. But given how fast science is moving and all that, one day we're probably going to know everything we need to know about it. So what about right here, all the black holes on this planet? There's so much that nobody can explain. Like, why does everyone run around thinking everything they do is so important? We're all going to die, so what does it matter if you get an A on a test or come in first or fiftieth place on the balance beam at some gym meet?

The real mystery to me is why we're born, why we die, and why we do what we do in between. As far as I can tell, nobody has answers for that.

People. That's the real final frontier.

After that, Tyler found himself looking up random words on Amanda's computer and printing out what he found. Something would pop into his head, and he wanted—needed—to find out if she had anything to say on the subject.

Under the word *God*:

Sometimes I feel like I'm the only one who sees real life—and everyone else is just a programmed pod person. But the next minute, I wonder what's wrong with me. Why is everyone else happy? Why do I feel like I'm missing something really, really important, like a personal text message from God?

Under *crying*:

I wonder if Tyler remembers the time I had poison oak so bad I thought I would die. I had it everywhere, on my scalp, between my toes, even you know where. Tyler heard me crying in the middle of the night and stayed up with me watching *101 Dalmatians.* The movie was his idea. Dogs with spots, me with spots. I'll never forget that.

Under *earth*:

People say to try and live every day like it's your last one on earth. But how do you do that when there's homework? You get in big trouble if you blow it off. But I bet no one dies saying, "If I could live my life all over again, I'd do more homework."

Under *life*:

Today, I tried to be aware of every moment of my life. Everyone thought I was acting really weird. Tyler asked what the hell I was staring at. It was impossible to take it all in. I thought I would explode.

Tyler had assumed that he had known everything about his sister, who she was, why she did what she did, the usual stuff that brothers know about their annoying little sisters. Now he wasn't sure. Who was this person who grappled with the same kind of questions that went through his own head? It was as if there were all these different girls bouncing around inside of her, up and laughing one minute, down and crying the next.

Who was she?

Did he want to know this person better?

If he knew her better, would he like her?

If he liked her, then what? What then?

If he knew her and if he liked her, something else might happen. He might love her.

And if you love someone and they aren't there anymore and there's no way to get them back, you miss them. You can't help it. You really, really miss them.

And he wouldn't just miss the Amanda who was fourteen and frozen in time. He would miss the Amanda who was seventeen and eighteen and twenty-five and thirty. He would miss the sister he was supposed to have his whole life, who would share his memories and know him in the way that nobody else did.

It takes a lot of courage to love something that death can touch—that death has already touched.

Tyler shuddered with the full understanding of what that sentence really meant. He was getting to know his sister, getting to love her, starting to miss her. That might lead to more than his heart could bear.

TWENTY-THREE

I GOT AN INFECTION and then another infection. None of them were life-threatening, but they kept me in the hospital. More tests and more IV drips and another round of tests. It seemed like I was never going to get to go home. That was the bad news. But with the bad came the good. On one of those hospital-bound days, I experienced two momentous events.

The first: Milo Nutley officially introduced me to his parents, a major step forward in our relationship. A thousand TV shows, movies, and dating Web sites can't be wrong. Meeting the parents labels you as more than *just friends*. Mom likes to say that labels are for pickle jars, but I don't think this is the kind of situation she has in mind. I think she was thrilled for me.

I had certainly seen the Nutley parents around the hospital before. Milo and his mom looked separated at birth, which of course they were. They had the same broad forehead and same gap between their front teeth. I've heard that a front-tooth gap signals a healthy sexual appetite, so why mess things up with braces? Milo obviously got his very masculine body type—long legs and broad shoulders—from his dad, but happily not the middle-age paunch flopping over his belt.

I knew that his parents weren't divorced and had never even been married to other people. That made them as boring as two old, tired dogs to Milo. To me, however, they were objects of fascination. Pretty much every adult of my acquaintance—serial daters like Beth and the other single moms in our apartment building—had cycled through every possible variation of coupledom. I could fill a wall with diagrams of arrows and circles of Mom's romantic entanglements. As a result, Mom, who's an optimist in every other area of life, frequently said bitter, uncomplimentary things about the institution of marriage. *That's why they call it an institution. A prison is an institution, too!*

A person of my age and with my nondating experience shouldn't have to hear negative stuff like that all the time. A person should get to experience the other side once in a while. So whenever I spotted the Nutleys in the hallway, I studied them extra hard. I noticed whenever a quick touch or glance passed between them. I basked in their presence, and not just because

Milo was the wonderful fruit of their loins. They possessed a secret I wanted. They knew how a man and a woman can remain uncheating and in love and keep their marriage alive, even when one of them has an unsexy belly paunch and the other should definitely add highlights to her lackluster hair.

I considered Milo's folks to be part of a rare, select group, akin to ospreys, pigeons, certain apes, termites, beavers, bald eagles, red-tailed hawks, and sand cranes, all of which, according to the Internet, mate for life and give me hope.

I had spent many happy moments envisioning my first official introduction to the Parents. Perhaps it would be in a fancy restaurant, Milo and me in our best clothes, our new healthy organs pumping and beating and secreting behind perfectly healed scars. I imagined ordering something definitely not recommended by the American Heart Association.

But as Mom says, life has this way of stomping its big foot onto the spine of the best-laid romantic plans. My introduction to the Parents took place right before the Pediatric Transplant Family Support Group in the all-purpose room on the fourth floor of Children's Hospital. No pâté, but there were carrot sticks and low-fat bran muffins. Mom was there. So were Wendy (who had already been sent home and was back for this special event) and her parents and the hospital social worker, plus a half dozen or so transplant wannabes. Some of the kids resembled me, with the telltale bushy eyebrows and chipmunk cheeks of the newly transplanted.

Before the support group got officially started, all the kids hung around self-consciously. Milo looked particularly awkward sitting by himself in a wheelchair on the other side of the room. Standing near him, his parents were engrossed in conversation with Wendy's mom and dad. I did notice with disappointment that at one point, Mr. Nutley's eyes wandered around the room and did a double-take when they landed on Mom, who looked especially gorgeous compared to all the pasty skin, bloated features, and stringy, dull hair in the room. I think Mrs. Nutley noticed, too. Without even pausing in the conversation, she pulled her husband closer, flashed her gap-toothed smile, and said something that made him look at her in appreciation.

Note to self: Don't sock your true love in the gut just because he gawks at a gorgeous stranger across a crowded room.

My eyes turned instinctively to Milo. I was just in time to catch him on the verge of having a similar moment with another girl in the room, the one with the new pancreas and the real cleavage. Somehow, she had done something fashionable with her hospital gown. She was batting her eyelashes so hard I thought she'd sprain the lids. Shameless. But I couldn't really blame her. Milo did happen to be the cutest boy in the room. Not that there was much competition. The only one who came even close had a funny-shaped, pointed head, which wouldn't have been a problem except that he had no hair due to some medical procedure that I prayed I would never have to have.

So, anyway. I didn't want Milo looking at that girl for too long, so I grabbed some carrots and crossed the room.

"Hey," I said.

"Hey," Milo said back.

"Carrot?"

"Sure."

I handed it to him. "Ever been to one of these things before?"

"Support group? Yeah. Sixty minutes of probing into how you feel. Sixty minutes of pressure to *share*. Sixty minutes of listening to everyone else *share*. It sucks."

"Totally."

"I'm only here because the social worker says attendance demonstrates compliance, and that's important if a liver match turns up. I need to prove I have a positive attitude because of my, um, previous transplant screw-up."

"Well, a positive attitude never killed anyone."

"What's that supposed to mean?"

"Not really sure. My mom says it about once a day."

"I hate these meetings, especially when someone in the group starts to cry."

I pointed across the room to the girl with cleavage. "She looks like a crier. Definitely."

"When someone cries, there's all this pressure to say the right thing. And then, inevitably, the group hug. First sign of a tear, and everyone is all over the crier." Milo winced. "Please don't let anyone cry today."

And that's when it happened, the introduction. I must give credit and a big thanks to Wendy for being her obnoxious, spoiled self. She realized that she had spent a whole three minutes without her parents' full attention focused only on her needs. I could have hugged her (but I didn't) when she started whining and nagging. Mrs. Nutley gave one of those weak smiles of sympathy and understanding that moms give each other. Wendy's dad shook hands with Mr. Nutley before picking up his daughter and heading over to the snack table.

The Nutleys now had only one place to turn. To Milo and me. I smiled at them. They smiled at me. I waited, my weight shifting from foot to foot. Mrs. Nutley touched her son's shoulder.

"Milo, why don't you introduce us?"

And just as though Milo always did exactly what his parents asked of him, just as if he personally thought this was the best idea in the world, he said, "Mom, Dad, this is Dani."

That was the first momentous event of the day. The second?

I held my own heart.

But hold on. Before I put hand to heart, there was the Pediatric Transplant Family Support Group meeting.

I didn't admit this to Milo, but I actually enjoy listening to people reveal their innermost feelings. I think most people do, or there wouldn't be so many soap opera addicts in the world. I also didn't mind the idea of talking about myself, as long as it stayed within the bounds of good taste. I had no intention of going into detail about post-transplant diarrhea. Some things are best kept to yourself.

We sat in a large circle, each kid flanked by one or two parents. The social worker, a man named Paul with the pointy ears of an elf, got things going by welcoming us in a very peppy way. We went around the circle and introduced ourselves quickly: name, age, body part, pre- or post-op. Parents tended to be more long-winded.

For example, there was Mother of David Who's Waiting for Lungs and Is So Incredibly Brave. There was Grateful Dad of Carrie Who Got a New Heart Three Months Ago and He's So Blessed to Have Her Home Again and Wants to Thank Every Nurse, Social Worker, and Doctor Who Crossed Their Path During This Long, Grueling Ordeal.

After getting the basics on each other, social worker Paul set out the ground rules of sharing, of which there were surprisingly many, such as *No offering unsolicited medical advice* and *Use "I" statements* and *What is said in this room stays in this room.* He held up something that he called a "talking stick" and acted like it had mystical powers of the American Indian sort. It was only one of those cheap back scratchers you buy as a souvenir in Chinatown.

"Whoever has the stick gets to talk uninterrupted," he explained. "Any questions about the rules and procedure?" Silence. "No? Good. So who wants to get us started?"

A cough. A nose blow. Silence, except for Wendy, who for insane reasons understood only by a spoiled eight-year-old, burst out singing "Doe, a deer, a female deer" from *The Sound of Music.* Her parents, who obviously found every annoying thing she did to be charming, didn't shush her or anything. Then she opened a shoe box and dumped lots of papers onto the floor.

"Get-well cards from all my friends!" She rummaged around and waved a sheet of paper in the air.

"This one's from Amelia. 'Dear Wendy, Teacher says you got a new kidney. We're studying about kidneys. I bet you can pee real good now. Pisssssssssssssssssss sssss.' And this one is from my best friend Rachel and has a picture of a kidney bean that's going la-la-la-la-la-la. And this one from my other best friend Rachel is really funny. There's a superhero Kidney Girl and she's—"

It's a good thing social worker Paul broke in. "Well, thanks for sharing, Wendy. That put a lot of upbeat, positive energy in the room. Anyone want to share on *that* topic? Christine!"

He walked across the circle and handed the back scratcher to the flirt with the new pancreas. She lowered her eyes and sighed deeply, pressing the stick to her chest, which was rising and falling as if she had just won some great honor and was trying to convince us that she was not only a genius, but modest as well.

"Faith," she said, and after a two-beat dramatic pause, added, "has carried me through the hard times."

"Faith in what?" the boy with the funny-shaped head asked.

"Why, Henry, faith in God, of course."

"Faith," the social worker repeated. "Does anyone else here have faith in anything?"

"Myself!" Henry blurted out, but then cringed because he realized he had broken rule number six and waited for Christine to hand him the stick. "Myself," he said again, this time without the spontaneity.

The stick went around the circle. Two more people in a row said "God" and three kids said "my parents" and one mother said "my son's will to live" and Wendy's father said "my daughter's spunky courage."

My mom said "karma," which needed to be explained because there were actually some people in the room who had never heard of it. Where have they been? Mom got all tongue-twisted trying to explain because karma is complex in an Eastern way of thinking and most of the people in the room clearly had Western minds. Mr. Nutley jumped in and helped out by summing up, "Karma is, basically, what goes around comes around." Mom smiled at Mr. Nutley, and he smiled back, and Mrs. Nutley moved closer to her husband.

After the fifth time someone said "God," Milo grew so squirmy I knew there'd be no holding him back. Before the woman next to him could say the *us* in *Jesus*, he grabbed the stick from her. "Hundreds of years of medical research. That's what I have faith in."

"Point well made, Milo," the social worker said.

"And antirejection medication."

"Many, many things to give us faith for the future."

"And know what else? Know what I *need* to have faith in? Right now, I need to have faith that some healthy person is about to die suddenly. Like this!" Milo snapped his fingers. "Someone who didn't have time to get used to the idea of dying, like we have. Someone who thought they had all the time in the world. I'm praying for that person's death."

"That's a terrible thing to pray for!" Christine said.

"It sounds like you feel guilty, Milo. Guilt's not an unusual feeling under these circumstances," the social worker said. "Does anyone else have these feelings? Guilt isn't—"

Milo tossed the back scratcher into the center of the circle. Clang on the floor and instantly claimed by Henry's father. "I'm gonna hang a left here, folks, and move on to a different topic. I am sick to death of the endless medical insurance hassles." Other parents mumbled in agreement.

"Henry, did you have something to say?" the social worker asked.

"Dating. That's my problem. No one—I mean no one—wants to be my girlfriend. They're afraid I'm gonna croak in the middle of a date."

"Pills," said one of the mothers. "How do you make sure your teenager takes all his pills?"

"I do hate the pills," the boy next to her confirmed.

"Me too," Carrie with a new heart said, and her father told her to not even *think* about not taking them, and she came back with "Don't tell me what to do. It's my body!"

"Golly, people! There are so many blessings. Don't be so negative. We have so much to be thankful for," Christine insisted.

A boy with post-transplant face bloat came back at her. His voice had a mushed, pained quality. "Golly gee, easy for you to talk, Ned Flanders. You didn't turn into a whale after your transplant. Or get mouth sores." He stuck out his tongue, which explained why he talked so weird.

"Yeah, Christine. And you didn't get cancer from the antirejection medication and then need chemo," Henry added. His hand tried to smooth back hair that wasn't there. "Being bald doesn't help with the dating situation."

"At least you got your transplant," the girl across from him snapped. "I might never get a kidney."

Christine again. "Think positive. Think of the great college admissions essay we'll all have. A transplant beats community service hands down."

Wendy screamed that she wanted to go home.

Clearly, things had gotten out of hand. A definite chill settled over the support group, which made what happened next a welcome relief, at first anyway. Milo laughed. Loud. This was unusual because he typically had more of an ironic, twisted-half-smirk sense of humor. The laugh started in his belly and burst out of his nostrils in a wet way that made Christine say, "Gross."

"Laughter, the best medicine," the social worker said. "Care to share what's so amusing, Milo?"

The space between his eyebrows bunched as he considered the offer. I saw his mind turn even further inward. "Skeletons," he said without much inflection. "Everywhere." He pointed to Wendy's mom. "A skeleton eating a bran muffin." He pointed at Henry's father and then at Henry. "A skeleton worrying about insurance and another skeleton worrying about a date for Saturday night. Skeletons with their legs crossed and skeletons scratching their heads and picking their noses."

"I wasn't!" Wendy shouted.

Milo laughed again, an actual *ha!* as his eyes settled on Christine. She went pale. "And a skeleton who thinks God can keep her flesh from rotting and her bones from turning into dust and blowing away."

Everyone was thinking the same thing: Milo had just turned into a psycho. I could see it in their eyes. Even the social worker was fumbling for the right thing to say. Milo's gaze moved steadily around the circle. When it landed on me, his mouth opened, then closed. Mom took my hand and squeezed it. Mr. Nutley placed a calming palm on his son's shoulder, but Milo whacked it away.

He tried then to back his wheelchair out of the circle and swivel it in the direction of the door. But there wasn't enough room. He kept banging it into the baseboard. "Shit!" he cursed.

To leave, he needed to pull back into the group, move clumsily forward, and cut a diagonal across the circle. The social worker put out an arm to stop him, but Milo shook him off and kept going. You could hear his hard, sarcastic laugh as he struggled to open the door. Finally, it opened and then slammed behind him.

Christine's face pinched in horror. Wendy shook her finger, pronouncing Milo to be "a very, very bad boy."

But they didn't know him.

They hadn't noticed what I saw in the corners of his eyes and in the tremble building at the sides of his mouth.

Nobody there knew Milo. They only thought they did.

One minute more and his laugh would have turned into something else, into what it really was. Opposite emotion, same intensity. He had to get out of that room. Fast. Before his eyes turned red and wet. Before all the future skeletons came toward him and sur-rounded him with a group hug.

TWENTY-FOUR

"THE PATHOLOGY DEPARTMENT KEEPS them around for tests." Brianna the nurse placed it on a silver surgical tray, then wheeled the cart close to me.

This is my heart. This was my heart.

When she said "make a fist," I clenched my fingers, felt the nails digging into my palms. "See the size of your fist? That's the size a healthy heart should be. And this old one of yours is what? Three times the size! In the world of hearts, big doesn't mean strong. This heart had to work overtime to keep you alive. Would you like to hold it?"

I wanted to.

I didn't want to.

I wanted to.

I didn't want to.

I unclenched my fist. Blood rushed back into

the fingertips; two had gone almost white from pressure.

Mom gave me an encouraging nudge with her shoulder. "Go on."

Nurse Brianna handed me a pair of purple rubber gloves.

I could do this. I think I wanted to. Yes, I wanted to. The rubber gloves tightened over each finger and snapped around my wrists.

I held my hands together like I was going to drink water from a stream. The muscles in my upper arms tensed with anticipation. My elbows dug into my sides. Afraid to move, certain that something terrible would happen if I did. What if I jostled the heart? Or dropped it?

"Relax," the nurse said. "This puppy isn't running off anywhere."

And then without any ceremony, as if it were the most common thing in the world, she placed my own heart in the palms of my own hands.

There.

I was holding it.

It wasn't slimy, more the texture of a rubber ball.

I waited for something. For what?

I expected to feel *something*, a sensation related to electricity. A shock, a twitch, a vibration. But there was nothing like that. There was just this weight in my hands, with no more connection to me than baby teeth after they had fallen out.

The heart had been biopsied and the two halves dropped apart like a cut piece of fruit, a firm peach maybe, only gray and rubbery. All the songs written about it, the poems, the greeting cards. Here it was, the core of a human being, the core of me. But there was no magic, no mystery. A wave of disappointment. I didn't know what I wanted to feel. Anything, I guess. Anything but *nothing*.

Mom was the one with the charge. Giggly and euphoric, she rocked back and forth heels to toes. "Dani, oh my gawd! How does it feel? I can't believe you're doing this."

"So, young lady, what are you thinking?" Nurse Brianna asked.

I couldn't think of anything to say, except a lame "it's cool."

"The coolest! Let me give you the guided tour."

My eyes followed her finger as she pointed out the specifics of everything that had gone wrong. I had to bend really close to see what she was talking about because even though this heart was huge and swollen by human heart standards, everything about it was so small. And so wrong.

Up until then, I guess there had been a part of me that still wondered if I had really needed a transplant.

Now the evidence sat in front of me. How everything was broken beyond repair.

How it had never been any good.

How it cheated me out of being a regular baby, a regular kid, a regular teenager.

How it failed me.

How I almost died.

Wendy had a name for her old kidneys. I finally had one for my old heart.

Humpty Dumpty.

Busted. Shattered.

The worst heart that any human being could be born with.

Now came the feelings, a flood of them. A sensation spread through me, hands to arms to shoulders to chest to throat to forehead, a surge that felt like it would explode and leave two giant holes where my temples used to be. Shame and horror that this thing had been cut out of my body. Anger.

I glared at the heart: *Do something! Beat!*

But why would it do that now? It had never done its job before. Never.

Who did this heart think it was?

I wanted to slap it and make it apologize for being the inferior, shoddy piece of body merchandise that it was. *Apologize!*

But no, it remained silent. I opened my hands and

let the heart drop a few inches back onto the tray. Drop, like the piece of raw meat that it was. "This is what happens when you don't do your job. You get sliced in half and stuck in a drawer."

"Whoa. Didn't expect that reaction," the nurse said.

I turned my back, didn't give a flying fart about that old Humpty Dumpty heart. "Put it in the garbage, for all I care."

"No!" Mom insisted. "Dani, I'm so grateful to your heart. It kept you alive so long. Please? Let me record this historic moment."

For Mom's sake, because I didn't ever like disappointing her, I picked it up again. She held up her cell phone and danced around trying to get the perfect angle. Finally, she snapped a picture and sent the image through the phone to everyone we knew. I wasn't smiling.

> Dear Donor Family,
>   I didn't hear back from you after my first letter. That's totally understandable. But to be honest, I'm kind of disappointed. No guilt trip intended. My mom and friend Milo said I should write down my thoughts and questions, even if I never go ahead and mail this letter.
>   So, okay.
>   I want to tell you about one day this week, the day I held my old, broken heart.
>   I guess there were a lot of choices of how I could

have felt about that. Excited. Nervous. Happy. Sad. Maybe a little grossed out, even though my extensive medical history has made me practically immune to that kind of thing.

But what I actually felt surprised me. And I don't totally understand it. I felt angry. And the anger still hasn't gone away. I'm not normally an angry kind of person, but I know enough to understand that you don't get this pissed off at something you don't care about. You can only be angry at something when it's connected to you, when it's part of you, when it still holds power over what and who you are.

So what I'm saying is that I must feel like that old busted heart still belongs to me. Even though it's sliced and diced and not beating and never beat very well to begin with. I guess I still consider it to be my heart.

So, then, whose heart is in my chest?

There's only one thing I do know about it: It's somebody else's heart. Heart of a Stranger.

But what stranger? Who?

I didn't send that letter either. The version I sent was more polite.

Dear Donor Family,

I want you to know that the heart continues to work beautifully. I imagine it came from a very beautiful person.

A week later, Mom brought in a letter that the transplant network had sent to her. It was addressed to *Dani. Heart Recipient*. When I opened it and unfolded the paper, it contained only two words: *Amanda Schecter*. The letters were slanted, big and loopy. This wasn't a parent who wrote back. I recognized the sloppy penmanship of a teenage boy when I saw it.

I had a name for my old heart. I now knew what to call this new one. Amanda's heart.

TWENTY-FIVE

HOSPITALS AREN'T BIG ON helping organ recipients snoop into the personal lives of their donors. They make sure any communication goes through proper channels. As you can imagine, there's high risk of an emotional meltdown. But Milo said on the phone, "Screw proper channels. We're not hurting anyone. It's my laptop. Come over after lunch."

It took me about an hour to decide what to wear. Jeans always look good, but what with them? I didn't have a lot of choices. There was the dorky striped turtleneck bought by Mom at some second-hand store. Or the gorgeous blue shirt that showed off my eyes but also showed off the top four inches of a raw, red scar. Lovely.

I changed back and forth three times. Then in complete fashion frustration, I buzzed for Nurse Joe. He was a guy, and I needed a guy's opinion, even a middle-aged one. "Glad this was an emergency." He studied the two choices. "In my humble masculine opinion, the blue."

"But what about . . . you know?"

"Dani, you can't wear turtlenecks the rest of your life. You earned that scar. Wear it proudly."

I still wasn't convinced, but went with the semi-plunging neckline. If anybody would appreciate the craftsmanship of my stitches, it would be Milo. With the letter from the donor family in my pocket, I dashed the short distance to his room. I had been doing my exercises on the rehab treadmill, and the results showed. Standing in his doorway, I didn't make a single unladylike, out-of-breath wheeze. That's how good I felt.

"Hey," I said.

"Hey, nice—" I waited for Milo to say *shirt* or *scar*, but his voice dropped and his eyes went back to the computer screen.

Awkward moment number . . . too many to count.

Would this feeling I got around Milo ever go away? I was suddenly self-conscious about everything—my bloated face, my hairy arms, the cold sores throbbing on the corners of my lips. I shifted right foot, left foot, right foot, left foot and coughed nervously into my fist. He looked up, confused, but then he caught on. I was relieved when he said, "Don't be such a dork," and pointed to the chair by his bed. I sat. He smelled nice, like soap and something else, which made me wonder if he had put on cologne especially for me.

On the computer screen, the search engine was all ready to go.

"Name," he said. "Spell it."

I opened the letter. "S-c-h-e-c-t-e-r. Amanda."

Milo typed, but as soon as his index finger moved toward the Enter key, panic kicked in. My hand darted out and tightened around his wrist. I thought I had wanted to know more about her, about Amanda. But now that it was a real possibility, I wasn't sure.

No! I was sure I *didn't* want to know. I wanted to go back and unsend those letters I wrote and undo the letter that came back. If I let Milo take this next step, it could never be undone. Like when you're a little kid and go to a lot of trouble to prove that the Tooth Fairy doesn't exist. You finally have the truth, but then you're not sure you want it. What have you really gained?

"What?" Milo said, sharp, annoyed.

"I don't want to know."

"You wrote the letters. Someone finally answered. Don't be a baby. What are you afraid of?"

"I'm not sure exactly. I—"

Milo shook off my wrist and tapped the Enter key.

My mouth dropped open at the hinge, and the word "don't!" rolled off my tongue. The whole world took on that slow-mo feeling. His finger pulling back slowly from the keyboard. His head swiveling toward me, like it was a science fair project demonstrating the principle of hydraulics. For what seemed forever, nothing changed on the screen. It was excruciating. But still, I knew that time—real time—was moving at its ordinary lightning speed. I could feel the evidence, the heart pounding away in my chest.

And then her name was everywhere.

She was real.

There was an article in the sports section of the local paper: Amanda Schecter flips and spins her way to the top score in the regional gymnastics meet. Amanda Schecter makes the eighth-grade honor roll. Amanda Schecter, one of three youth volunteers at the Humane Society, honored for two hundred hours of community service.

"It's so strange," Milo said. "When you die, you're not here anymore. But your MySpace profile lives on forever."

He clicked on the MySpace link, and my eyes dashed madly around the screen, grabbing on to words and icons, names and pictures. Her favorite music. Her best friends. Photos. Is that her? Her wall was filled with messages:

Amanda, we'll miss you!
Amanda, you were the best!
Amanda, I will never, ever, ever forget you.

The whole page seemed to buzz, each new piece of information about Amanda humming a different note in a different key. No melody, no harmony, just all these different clashing sounds trying to be heard, trying to come together as a whole.

Who was she?

I couldn't take it anymore. I reached across Milo's lap, and before he could stop me, I clicked off the site. I shut my eyes, sank back into the chair. A moment later, he said, "One more?" He didn't wait for my answer.

"It's the obit in the local paper. Beloved daughter of Robert and Claire, sister of Tyler, died today—"

"Stop!" I ordered, my eyes squeezed closed.

"There's a picture of her."

"I don't want to see it. I can't."

> *Dear Tyler (That is your name, right?),*
> *Wow, Amanda sounds like an amazing person.*
> *Really amazing.*
>
> *I guess that's all I planned to say in this letter, and then thank you again and sign off.*
>
> *But I can't stop there because . . . I don't know why exactly. I need to say this to somebody, and I picked you, which doesn't make sense because I don't*

TWENTY-SIX

FOR TYLER, RETURNING TO school was miserable. His first few weeks back, kids and teachers he didn't even know made a big fuss over him or, worse, went silent and awkward when he walked by. *That's him, the brother of the dead girl.* His new identity.

But then a couple of juniors almost died from overdoses and the big buzz immediately shifted from Amanda. In a perverse way, Tyler actually felt grateful to those kids. The pressure was off. He could go back to being just Tyler, pretty much anonymous and forgettable. He noticed with a sinking sense how the horror of his sister's death simply faded in the bloom of another horror. Tragedy replaced tragedy, like they were nothing more than a series of TV shows. The same kids who had been hugging and crying and whispering about Amanda were now high on this latest drama, desperate to fill up the shallowness and boredom of their own lives. It made Tyler feel disgusted and more disconnected from people than he usually felt.

Each day, the minute his last class let out, Tyler headed directly home. At least the house was empty. His mother had gone back to teaching, and she immediately buried herself in her class and students, staying as late as possible at school to grade papers and make lesson plans. Tyler opened the front door, tossed his backpack on a chair before checking the mail. There was a large envelope from the transplant network. He knew what was in it.

Upstairs in his room, he locked his door even though no one was home.

Dear Donor Family,

My name is Jermaine and I'm in eleventh grade. Because of you, I have a new liver, and a new life.

I was born with biliary atresia. That means that the bile—which is basically a stream of toxic waste—couldn't drain out of my liver. When I was only a couple of months old, doctors gave me an operation, but we knew it wouldn't keep me alive forever. While I was waiting for a transplant, my liver got so bad it couldn't break down food at all. I had to be fed liquid mush through a tube. That's as gross as it sounds.

Because of your gift, I have a real life now. I want to say thanks, even though that's kind of lame. You deserve a lot more than that, but I can't find the right words. So the thanks coming your way has horns and drums and a big opera singer belting it out. I hope you hear it loud and clear, and that it gives you at least a little bit of comfort.

> *Sincerely yours,*
> *Jermaine, your loved one's*
> *liver recipient*

Dear Donor Family,
My daddy got new lungs. He's a firefighter. You saved his life. You saved mine, too! I couldn't live without my daddy.

> Love and kisses,
> Emily, age six

P.S. My mom helped me write this letter. She says thanks, too. That makes three lives saved. Plus anyone my dad saves in a fire.

To My Donor Family,
My name is Jaya, and I'm twelve. At the age of four, I was diagnosed with diabetes.

I tried to write you a letter five times since my transplant, but I never got very far before I started crying. I feel bad about not getting in touch sooner. I just want to get this down on paper. Thank you, thank you for the pancreas.

I also want to say how sorry I am for the loss of your family member. It's not easy to decide to donate an organ. I know because when I was eleven, the diabetes first wrecked my kidneys and my dad gave me one of his. That means we're a donor family, too.

No one can ever replace your loved one, but I hope it makes things a little easier knowing that there's someone who no longer has to take injections or check their sugar ten times a day. I can eat whatever I want. I can think about going to college, maybe becoming a doctor. I am so grateful to be just a normal kid.

I need to stop writing now because I'm crying again.

Yours truly,
Jaya (which means Victory)

TWENTY-SEVEN

THE FRONT DOOR OPENED. His mother's voice: "Tyler?"

"In my room."

"Come down and say hi. How was your day? Any mail?"

"On the kitchen table."

A pause. "This magazine? That's it?"

Every day, the same question hung in the air. His mother's voice expectant, then that note of disappointment. Tyler kept hearing what his mother would probably deny if he pointed it out to her. She was waiting for something miraculous that would undo or make sense of Amanda's death.

Tyler didn't answer her.

He looked at the final letter and recognized the handwriting on the envelope. From her. From Dani.

From the girl with his sister's heart. He took his time reading her letter twice, turned on Amanda's computer, and Googled the few facts that he had: Dani and heart transplant and high school and the name of their town.

It didn't take long to track her down. A few months earlier, there had been a neighborhood fund-raiser to help pay her hospital bills. The local weekly newspaper published an article. From that, Tyler learned her last name, and her mother's name, and the school she went to, and the name of the neighbor organizing the event. A hundred people had attended. He learned the amount of money raised and how she had been born with her heart on the wrong side of her chest and that she played soccer once and liked old, scary movies. He learned that she didn't live far away. Not far at all. He wouldn't even need to take a bus. He could bike there in no time, if he wanted to.

But why would he want to do that? What would that prove? Would he knock on her door? Would she open it? If she did, what would he say? What would she say? What would he say back? He would probably just stand there. And she would stare, and it would all be a big, big mistake.

Tyler ordered himself to put the idea out of his mind. It was pointless. He tried to click off the newspaper site, but nothing happened. Frozen. Then the screen flashed once before going dark. When he tried to reboot, nothing. Nothing at all.

Amanda's computer was old. Maybe it could be fixed. Or maybe the hard drive had crashed and with it her private thoughts, her secret wishes, the memories the two of them had shared. He felt relieved that he had printed some of the documents.

His sister had already died once. He couldn't lose her again.

In the middle of the night, Tyler bolted upright in bed. What was it? Why did he keep thinking about this girl Dani? He had nothing to tell her. There wasn't a string of questions he wanted to ask her. He didn't care about this girl's favorite subject at school or what music she liked or even what she thought about the big things like God or death.

So what was it? What was the pull? What did Tyler need?

The answer came to him as one of those strange expressions that he would normally never use.

To lay eyes on her.

"I need to," he said aloud.

That was an understatement. He needed to see her in the way that the earth needed to revolve around the sun.

Tyler had all the traits of a good spy. He could be patient when he wanted to be. He knew how to dig up information and how to pretend that everything was normal. He was very sneaky. He had a whole child-hood's worth of experience in that. So the next morning, he woke, brushed his teeth, went to school, zoned out in class, felt contempt for everyone around him, came back home, grabbed his bike, and headed off.

It took a while to find Dani's place because it wasn't an easy-to-identify house but an apartment in one of those low-slung complexes that sprawls like the arms of an octopus around a central rental office. He didn't even have her specific apartment number. Frustrating. Her letters didn't give any clue about hair color or height, anything that could help pick her out.

So he decided to suck up the nerve to ask. There were two preteen boys on skateboards; they buzzed by too fast. He ruled out a group of kids about his own age smoking by a clump of trees. Too much attitude. Then two girls—looked like about sixth grade—made things easy by coming right up to him.

"Are you new here? You're new here." They looked like they had been shopping at yard sales and decided to wear everything at once, hippie skirts and polka-dotted leggings and berets and vests with metal studs and mis-matched earrings and weird high-top camo sneakers.

"How do you know I'm new?"

The one with the bright yellow shawl answered. "We know everyone. We're the fashion setters of this place."

"We especially know all the boys."

"I'm just visiting. Actually, I'm looking for, um, my friend. Her name is Dani."

"Dani!" one shrieked, and the other asked, "Who wants to know? If she's really your friend, you'd know she's in the hospital."

"Is she okay?" he blurted, and then scrambled for a more casual tone. "I didn't know because I'm an out-of-town friend. I mean I was out of town, but now I'm here."

"She was supposed to come home, but then she got an infection, and now the infection is getting better. I think she might be home soon, maybe the end of the week. Are you a *boy*friend?"

"No, I'm . . . a boyfriend would know her apartment, right? So I'm not because . . . which one is it?"

Yellow shawl pulled on his sleeve, and he followed them across the courtyard. They pointed to a blue door that looked like all the other blue doors. He felt strange about that. It was supposed to look somehow different. Parked in front was an old Toyota with rusted red paint. Tyler jutted his chin at it. "And that's—"

"Her mom's car. So, aren't you going to knock?"

"You said she wasn't home."

"You could leave a message. A *love* message."

"It's got to be weird."

"What?" Tyler asked.

"Knowing someone died so you could be alive."

Tyler felt something squeeze in his chest. For some reason, he needed to defend this girl he didn't know. "She—Dani—didn't do it. . . . You know, she didn't kill anyone."

"Yeah, guess not. But it's got to be weird."

"Creepy," agreed the other.

From a far end of the complex, a mom voice yelled and the girls ran off. Tyler returned their "see ya!" then turned his attention back to the apartment door. Nothing going on. And now the kids who were smoking were checking him out. Yeah, they were suspicious, all right. He better take off. Nothing more would happen today anyway. Dani was still in the hospital.

Tyler hopped on his bike, and when he circled around toward the exit, he caught a glimpse of a woman coming out of the apartment. He got off his bike and pretended to check a tire. She draped the front door with some orange party streamers and tacked up a handwritten sign: WELCOME HOME. With a red marker, she added DANI!

The next day, Tyler cut class before lunch. When he got to the apartment complex, no one was around. Anyone who would have recognized him from yesterday must be in school. Good. Still, he better not just stand in the middle of the courtyard. He headed over to the clump of trees and picked an oak toward the back. From that angle, he could see the apartment door clearly. But unless someone was specifically looking for him, Tyler knew he blended in. If anyone spotted him at all, he was just some high school boy chilling out with a book.

He kicked aside some cigarette butts, sat down, got comfortable. Who knew when she'd be getting home? It could be hours.

TWENTY-EIGHT

"PROMISE?"

"Promise."

I assured Milo that I would visit him. And when I couldn't get to the hospital, I'd call. Every day. But that wasn't the promise he kept talking about. No matter how hard I tried to keep the conversation about *us*, about the future of us, he kept coming back to her. The heart donor. *Her*. Amand. . . . It was impossible for me to say her name aloud anymore; it lodged in my throat. It was hard to even hear someone else say it. It made her too real, too much of a person. But Milo kept going on and on about how he wanted to know more about her. He wanted me to be the one to find out. And no matter how much I tried not to, I felt these strange pangs of jealousy. But at the same time, I felt ridiculous and pathetic because there was no one to be jealous of.

"Why is this so important to you?"

He fumbled to put his thoughts together. "It's maybe . . . not important for me, but for you."

"It's not important to me."

"You might not think that now. But if I knew more about the guy whose liver I got, maybe I wouldn't have treated it so—"

"That's you. I'm me. I don't . . ."

My voice trailed off. It was hard to get self-righteous with someone who looked as awful as Milo did. Those dark circles under his eyes. His stomach was so bloated he could have been hiding a cantaloupe under his top. Another sign that his liver was shutting down. How could I argue?

So I wound up promising that I would find out more about her. I really didn't think it was a promise I could keep. The thought of knowing anything more . . . why? Why did I have to know?

Why? Why? Why?

The truth—and this might sound selfish, but I don't care!—was that I wanted to know less. It wasn't that I wasn't grateful. *Thank you, thank you, thank you.* How many more times could I say that? I *was* grateful. But I wanted to wave a magic memory wand and forget about her for a while. Forget how she died. Forget that she had parents and a brother and friends, and how awful they must feel and how they'd never get over it, never stop missing her. How could they? Forget about all the things in life that she'd never get to do.

I wanted to forget that my heart, my real heart, was in some drawer in cold storage. I didn't want to keep thinking about that. I wanted to forget.

But I couldn't. I was reminded of her every time I talked to Milo and felt my heart speed up, every time it slowed down when I was drifting off to sleep. Why did I need to know anything more? I already felt her like a ghost wandering through every part of me, haunting me all the time. I wondered if I would ever *not* feel her.

"Ready to leave this joint for good?" Nurse Joe asked.

"Ready."

Dr. Alexander said that my latest echocardiogram was spectacular. That's the word she used. *Spectacular!* I had zero rejection of the heart and no infection anywhere. But still, due to insane insurance rules, I wasn't allowed to be a normal person and walk out of the hospital. Joe pushed the wheelchair, making jokey race car sounds. I guess he forgot that I wasn't eight. Dr. Alexander and Brianna, my other favorite nurse, walked alongside, carrying my suitcase and a packet containing a week's supply of pills and my hospital discharge instructions. The automatic door whooshed open, and Mom was waiting at the curb with the car.

Joe hugged me, and Mom hugged Dr. Alexander,

and Brianna got teary and then Joe did, too. It was like a math problem: *There are five huggers, some of whom are crying some of the time. How many permutations of hugging and crying can there be?*

We went through them all and then I buckled myself in. Joe leaned his elbow on the roof of the car and lectured me through the open window. "I don't want to see you back here ever again. Except for your regular checkups. Or to visit me. Or Milo."

"Take care of that heart. Promise?" Brianna asked.

"Promise."

After a couple of miles, I pointed out to Mom that we were headed in the wrong direction.

"For home it's wrong."

"Where are we going, then?"

Mom pulled the car into the next strip mall parking lot and shut off the engine. She stared down at her hands like someone caught cheating on a test. It wasn't like her to not meet my eyes. "Dani, I couldn't stop myself. I found out where they live. I thought you might . . . if you don't want to . . . I understand. No pressure. I'm not going to talk to them or anything. I just want to look, see. I thought . . ." Big sigh. "I'm not sure *what* I thought."

First Milo, now Mom. I didn't want to go. I didn't understand why she was so obsessed with *her*. "But why—"

Mom broke in because she knew exactly what I was going to ask. That's how insanely close we were. Usually, there was something great about not having to explain myself to someone and to have a mom who talked to me like we were best friends, practically inside each other's heads. But closeness like that could also be suffocating, and now was one of those times.

"It's this way, Dani. I know everything about you—who your father was, what you ate as a baby, everything that's gone into making you *you*. And now there's this other thing, this heart, and it's part of you. Where did it come from? *Who?* I need to know. Understand?"

I did, kind of, but I didn't care what she needed. I wanted her to start the car. I would stick my head out the window and take big, gulping lungfuls of air as we pulled away and went home.

I didn't care what she wanted!

And then I felt bad for not caring.

And then I felt angry that I felt bad. And then guilty for being angry.

I felt that heart speed up and start beating hard. I wanted to pound my fists on the dashboard, but I didn't. Our old, familiar mother-daughter dynamic kicked in and something collapsed inside me. Trapped.

She waited and when I gave her a weak nod and an even weaker smile, she asked, "Sure?"

"Sure."

But I wasn't. Not at all.

"That one?"

"That one."

We found the address no problem and parked across the street, far enough so we didn't look like we cared about that particular house, but close enough to see anyone coming or going. Mom had obviously given this parking plan a lot of thought. I don't know why she bothered. We looked like a perfectly normal mom and daughter parked on a street talking about mom-daughter stuff. When a man walked by with his dog, I made sure to look repentant like I was being lectured about breaking a major family rule.

The house. So there it was. The shingles were painted deep sky blue. Flowers in terra-cotta pots on the steps. A brass knocker on the brick-colored front door. The house was a lot nicer than anyplace Mom and I ever lived in, a real mom-dad-kid house, the kind I usually envied. I supposed Milo lived in one just like it. It looked like an ordinary house filled with people living ordinary lives. But it was anything but that. It was *her* house.

Outside, nothing was moving. No front door opened. No mail carrier arrived. The house had two stories, so I figured that the bedrooms—*her* bedroom and Tyler's—were upstairs. I quickly lowered my eyes, afraid of spotting any kind of movement at the windows, any sign of life. I wasn't ready for that.

Ten minutes passed, and I felt tense every second of it.

Then another ten minutes. Usually Mom and I never ran out of things to talk about. I don't think we'd ever been together in that small a space with so few words passing between us.

A half hour, and then finally I started to relax. Nothing was going to happen. They weren't home. They weren't coming home. I closed my eyes for a bit, and when I opened them, lacy curtains in a downstairs window fluttered once from a breeze. That was all, and I was really glad. Mom had gotten her chance to see the house. It was time to go.

"Beth, can we . . . ?"

That's when a silver Toyota pulled into the driveway. I took a breath and let it out only when the car door opened and a pair of legs in a skirt came out. Then hips, waist, shoulders, body, back of head. A mom, a regular mom coming home from a regular day at work. The only odd thing was how she stood there awhile looking at the house, studying it, like she was afraid of it. Then she whipped around so suddenly, I jolted and ducked my head so that it was resting on Mom's lap.

"Don't worry. She can't see us."

That's not what I cared about. I didn't want to see her. I didn't want to know if she had big teeth or a small, narrow mouth, if her eyes were wide-set or bunched in the middle of her face. I didn't want that face in my memory. If I knew what she looked like, I would always be looking for her, scared of seeing her every time I went into a store or walked down the street.

With my head on her lap, Mom began narrating the scene, stroking my hair like she was telling me a bed-time story.

"She's taking a briefcase out of the trunk. And she just slammed it closed. Now she's heading up the front walk."

I heard the beep of car doors locking.

"She's opening the front door and she's . . ."

I waited for Mom to continue, but she didn't. I didn't hear the sound, but I could tell by the way her stomach muscles fluttered that she was crying softly.

I guess I was, too.

It was almost dark now. We were about to leave when I heard the sounds. The click of a derailleur, the squeal of brakes. A boy on a bike made a wide turn into the driveway and disappeared into the shadowy space between the Toyota and a stand of rosebushes. He must have activated a sensor because two outdoor floodlights snapped on. Before I could look away, he removed his helmet.

Dark hair, a straight nose in profile. That's all I saw, but I knew. I knew for sure.

"The brother?" Mom asked.

"The brother."

"Tyler?"

"Tyler."

He rang the doorbell and said something to whoever answered. A moment later, the garage door opened from the inside. The boy walked in with his bike, both of them swallowed by darkness.

TWENTY-NINE

EVERYBODY MEANT WELL. I kept reminding myself of that. Before my transplant, our neighbors, some teachers, and people Mom worked with held a fundraiser to help with my humongous medical bills. Now they were holding a *Welcome Home, Dani* party, complete with heart-shaped balloons and heart-shaped cookies, and lots of music with a heart theme. Someone actually brought a heart-shaped meatloaf for the potluck. Wendy showed up, too, face bloated and hairy, but not self-conscious at all. She barged right in the front door.

"Close your eyes and hold out your hands," she ordered me. "I made it myself. Do you have a present for me, too? You should! You can open your eyes now."

My present from her was red and made of cloth. I think it was a pillow. It kind of looked like a pillow. At that moment, I realized there was going to be an endless parade of ugly, useless heart-shaped gifts in my future. I knew I was supposed to be grateful for every single one, plus gracious and totally unselfish to all the guests. I was supposed to answer every single personal question and keep smiling and saying thank you and telling everyone how great I felt and how much I appreciated all their effort and support.

More or less, that's what I did. The truth was more complicated and less smiley. The truth I saved for Milo. After a couple of hours of Wendy and hugs by strangers and neighbors pretending they didn't notice that my face resembled the moon in a children's book, I started to melt down. I sneaked away from my own party and locked the door to my bedroom. Milo picked up on the second ring.

I launched in. "There are these two insane sixth-grade girls who live in my same courtyard and keep following me around like news reporters. *But someone died for your heart. How does that feel?* I guess they mean well, but I want to slug them."

"Just because people mean well doesn't mean you owe them your soul. Boy, am I glad there's not a lot of songs about livers. Are there any?"

"I Left My Liver in San Francisco."

"Good one."

There was one of our awkward silences, so I filled it

with "Any news about—." I started to say "your transplant," only I remembered how much I hated it when people kept asking me. I wanted to rewind the conversation and take back the question. "News about, you know?"

Milo told me to count to ten.

"In English? I can do it in French, too."

"That works."

When I got to *dix*, his voice rose: "Hallelujah!" He sounded like a TV evangelist. "Seven people were just born. Now count to thirteen."

I did it—"*treize*"—and his voice dropped: "Lament. Ten people just died."

I wasn't sure what to say.

"Hallelujah!"

I still didn't know what to say.

"Lament. . . . So that's what I've been doing all day."

"Counting?" I asked.

"Weird, huh? The nurse even double-checked my meds, but there's nothing wrong. I could have told him that. I can't stop thinking about these statistics I read. Every ten seconds, someone is born and there's all this happiness for some people. Every thirteen seconds, a death and sadness for others. I mean, what do you do with information like that?"

"Unless one or the other is happening to you, I guess you don't even notice."

"Yeah, most of the time we just eat and sleep and basically sleepwalk through life. I can't get over that. All these missed opportunities."

"To feel really good. Or really bad."

I thought the next silence meant that Milo was counting, but I didn't hear the *hallelujah* I expected: "I might have some news," he said.

"News?"

"I can try to transmit it to you. Like before, mind to mind through the phone line."

"Really? A liver?"

"They can't ever be sure until the last minute. You know that. But they say it might be a good match."

There was a knock at my bedroom door. A *knock* is putting it mildly. If door knocking was an Olympic sport, this person was going for the gold, bringing one home for the USA.

"Go away!" I yelled.

"Huh?" Milo asked.

"Not you."

From the other side of the door: "Dani, Dani, who you talking to?"

"Your boyfriend?"

It was the two sixth-graders in the crazy clothes, followed by the dreaded Wendy voice: "Her boyfriend is Milo." Smooching sounds. "I know everything. Dani and me are organ sisters."

"Beat it!" I shouted.

Wendy must have told them her insane theory about us now being related, because there was a shout of overlapping "ewwww" and "gross" and more banging on the door.

"Who's there?" Milo asked. "Is that who I think it is?"

"Yes, it's Wendy!" To the door: "Stop it! Now!" Back to the phone: "They are such jerks!"

And then Mom's voice: "Have you girls seen Dani?"

"She's in there! She won't answer! The door's locked."

Mom's voice in panic mode. "Dani! Honey! Are you okay?"

From the receiver: "Better go back to your party."

"They'll break down the door if I don't." Before I hung up, I counted and said "lament" and waited until Milo counted and said "hallelujah!" I wanted to end the phone call on a good note.

One by one, the guests left, leaving behind deflated balloons, dirty paper plates, and cookies that were no longer heart-shaped but smashed and ground into the carpet. Mom, in her role as Superwoman, insisted she didn't need help cleaning up. A couple of neighbors insisted that she did. The cleanup crew got to work tackling the mess while I went outside to get some air.

It was late afternoon, with the sun making long, yellow slants across the courtyard. I was tired. I sat in our old lawn chair and watched some girls jumping rope and listened to the vacuum going full-blast inside. I folded in half the pillow Wendy made and tucked it under my head. It was pretty comfortable after all.

Relax. That's what I needed to do. Dr. Alexander insisted relaxation was crucial for my recovery. The social worker had shown me his favorite meditation technique, which involved sitting back, lowering my eyelids, following my inhales and exhales, and letting any thoughts, emotions, and problems just drift into oblivion.

That sounds a lot easier than it is. You wouldn't think doing nothing could be so hard. The problem was that my mind is like a pinball machine with lights flashing and numbers twirling and my thoughts pinging around like a metal ball, bouncing from one thing to another, or sometimes getting stuck in the same spot again and again and again.

So while I was trying to follow my inhales and exhales, I kept imagining all those people being born and all those people dying. At ten breaths, I raised my arms overhead and shook them in a hallelujah-jazz-hands kind of way. I counted thirteen breaths and covered my face in grief, imagining an exhale that never rounded the corner to become the next inhale.

What *do* you do with information like that?

Inhale, exhale, inhale, exhale. I got lost in the repetition, in the roller coaster ride of sadness and happiness. I hallelujah-ed and lamented until it got dark and the volunteer crew left and Mom yelled, "Dani! Time to come in."

I covered my face for the unknown people who just died. Then I threw my arms in the air. *Please, let Milo get a liver! Please!*

Exhale. *Amanda.*

Inhale. *My own second chance.*

I felt a chill as the night breeze played on the hairs of my arms.

THIRTY

THE PARTY WAS ENDING. Tyler spotted the two giggling sixth-grade girls walking across the courtyard. He probably should leave too before someone saw him in the hiding place among the trees. He had seen what he had come to see. At least, he thought he had seen her. It must have been her. A girl had come to the door every once in a while and was hugged by a new guest. Every glimpse went through him like an electric shock.

But now the front door opened again. It was late afternoon with a harsh slant of sunlight. He had to squint against the brightness to get a good look as she settled into a lawn chair.

Medium height, kind of skinny. A really round face. Thick eyebrows. What else? Dark hair pulled back in a clip. She was so ordinary. It was disappointing. She shifted in the chair, and he thought he could see the top of a scar peeking out from the collar of her shirt. It surprised him how relieved that made him feel. She wasn't *just* a girl. She had a mark that everyone could see, something that set her apart. But the light shifted, and now he wasn't sure he saw anything. It could have been only a shadow.

That was when she started doing something strange. It was so random. She threw her hands in the air and waved them around. Just as suddenly, she collapsed, face into her hands, and looked so sad that Tyler wondered if she was crying. A few more beats and her hands shot happily into the air again.

Bizarre. Weird. Tyler felt vaguely embarrassed, like he was spying on something really private. Warmth moved into his cheeks. Yet he couldn't move his eyes away from her mysterious, goofy dance.

When the front door opened again, a group of women piled out, talking, laughing, calling "'bye, Dani." Next he heard a voice from inside the apartment. The girl glanced up, did her dance one more time. Face down, hands up. She stood.

She shivered then and wrapped her arms around her own shoulders. It was the most ordinary movement by an ordinary girl on an ordinary afternoon. But it did something to Tyler, touched him in a way he couldn't really describe. This was why he had come. This was what he needed to see. This ordinary girl. As she was. Simple, complex, alive.

Dear Organ Recipient,

Tell me what you did today. Don't spare any details. Doesn't have to be earthshaking. I'm a teenager, so you don't have to be formal or have perfect grammar.

From,

Tyler, brother of your donor

Dear Tyler,

You have to guess the earthshaking thing I did today. A, B, C, or D? Hold this letter upside down for the secret answer at the bottom. But don't cheat and look first.

A. Got in trouble in school cause me, Rachel, and Rachel passed notes in class. The teacher called me the gang leader. Tee-hee-hee. I was.

B. Threw up after this gross boy dared me to eat five servings of tapioca pudding.

C. Gave my new kidney a name. It's Seraphina. She's a girl/ballerina/good witch/kidney.

D. Took my old kidney to school for
   show-and-tell. It's in a plastic bag,
   and the hospital says I have to give
   it back.
Guess now! That's an order.
Love, Wendy

Answer: whatever you guess is wrong! I
did all four! I win!

Dear Tyler,
Today I blew out fourteen candles (the extra
one for good luck). I know this isn't a big deal for
most people, but for the first time in my life, I
got to eat a big piece of my own birthday cake.
Vanilla with almond buttercream frosting. I got
some good presents, too. But your gift, my
pancreas, was the best gift I've ever gotten.
             Love, Jaya

To Tyler—
Jermaine here with an answer to your question.
I went to school and aced a history test. Then
after school, I kinda had a fight with my new
girlfriend (name: Charlotte) because she thought
I said I'd meet her somewhere, only I said I'd
meet her somewhere else. So then Charlotte and
I made up and I got a haircut and watched some

TV and worked on my chem lab report. I'd been putting that off forever, so it was now or never. Is this the kind of stuff you want to hear about?

For dinner, Mom made chicken tacos and my sister decided suddenly to be vegan and I got caught in the middle of a fight between Mom and her. Not really a fight, more of a loud philosophical argument about animal torture, which made the chicken tacos a little less appetizing. I scarfed them down anyway. I'm a big guy; I need my protein.

So that was the day. Pretty regular. Nothing earthshaking to report, but it's all good. Mostly I want you to know I'm taking my pills. Every day. I'm eating healthy stuff and not letting myself get too tired out. The doc says I need to listen to my body. Not exactly sure what that means, but I do know who I'm not listening to—anyone who tells me to loosen up and have a beer.

I hope this information helps you. Maybe it will make you feel a little less sad. Know this: I'm taking super good care of the liver, like it's not just my own.

> Yours truly,
> Jermaine

Dear Tyler and other family who gave my
daddy his lungs—
Daddy still has to rest a lot. He can't
be a firefighter yet. Today he turned
the jump rope for me. I did eight
without missing.
Love, Emily

My Dear Tyler,
Six weeks and counting. That's when
my first great-grandchild will come into
the world. Which brings me to your
question about my day. I spent it
shopping for the baby. I found the
smallest booties you've ever seen, some
darling onesies, and a stuffed animal I
couldn't resist.

I also bought some yarn. I know
what's expected of a great-
grandmother, and I plan on living up to
the cliché. The yarn is bulky, the hook
thick. Thanks to your family, I have my
one good eye. This baby will get the
hand-crocheted blanket by Great-
grandma that she deserves.

So Tyler, brother of my donor, such
was my day. Is this the kind of thing

you're looking for? You said it doesn't have to be earthshaking, but it was an earthshaking day to me. Thanks to you, they all are.

> With so much appreciation,
> Miriam P.

THIRTY-ONE

THE LATEST CALL FOR Gus Sanchez's services came at the beginning of the school day when he was dropping off his son Miguel. His cell phone rang; he pressed his index finger to his lips, a reminder to Miguel to not talk while Daddy conducted urgent business.

"Sanchez," he announced into the phone.

At the entrance to Children's Hospital, he was met by a familiar face. As Gus unbuckled the cooler holding the liver, he said what Miguel had urged him to ask: "And this is for—?"

"Milo," said the nurse.

Gus repeated the name with a sense of deep satisfaction.

THIRTY-TWO

WHEN YOU ALMOST DIE and some combination of luck and timing and blood type gives you a second chance, you see things differently than most people. You've experienced parts of life that usually stay hidden beneath the surface of normal good health. The horrors of life; the amazing wonders of it.

I had been exactly where Milo was, so I knew all the things *not* to say to him. Like how great he looked. Let his other visitors pretend that he wasn't as pale as oatmeal, with drool congealing in the corners of his mouth. I also knew not to blather on about how perfect his life was going to be from now on. He'd be getting plenty of that from the optimistic well-wishers. We both knew all about the infections, mouth sores, and unsightly hairiness, along with the lifetime of pills.

There was also this other fact nobody liked to

mention. Secondhand organs don't last as long. Infection and rejection are always right around the corner. Chances are, neither of us would live to a ripe old age, and whenever I started thinking about that . . . well, that's why I'd never talk about life being perfect to Milo.

"I'm here," I said.

"You're here," he whispered back.

"So, what do you remember?"

"I remember the operating room was cold. Maybe it was the happy juice, but I wasn't nervous. I just felt numb. It was like I had lost even the fear of losing everything. Nothing left to hold on to. I remember thinking, this is where they fix me, or kill me."

"Did you do what you promised me?"

Isn't that the most Milo question you ever heard? It was only a few days after his transplant, and his eyes were finally staying open for more than ten minutes at a time, and that's the first thing he asked. He had a brand-new liver, but he still had his same old one-track mind.

"I did," I said.

"You found out more about her, about your donor?"

"Yes."

"And?"

"And . . . this came from the transplant network. It's from her brother."

I showed him the large manila envelope with my name written in black marker on the outside.

"What's in it?"

"I don't know. I didn't have the guts to go through it by myself. My mom offered to . . . but I . . . since it was your idea and everything, I decided to wait."

"So what are you waiting for?"

I undid the metal clip and peered inside.

Where to start?

I cleared a corner of Milo's bed, careful not to disturb any of the tubes draining fluid from his body. Then I dumped the contents of the envelope, a mess of papers, onto his blanket. There was a small, sealed white envelope—READ THIS FIRST—and a typed, half-page letter inside that began: *So you wanna know about Amanda. . . .*

I read it aloud. Milo's eyes closed, but he didn't drift off into Painkiller Land. I knew he was paying careful attention because of the sounds of surprise at the appropriate parts. It was an amazing letter, and not because of any college-level vocabulary or fancy turns of phrases. I don't mean any disrespect when I say that Tyler wasn't the best writer in the world. I mean, best in the traditional school-writing sense. In every other sense, this was the most perfect half-page letter that I had ever gotten in my life, perfect because it was both a total surprise and exactly what I had been waiting for.

I guess I could go on and on about who my sister was, but that would be just me interpreting. It would be more about me than anything else. So I decided to let Amanda speak for herself.

That's what all the enclosed papers were about. They were documents from her computer, printouts of what appeared when he searched for the word *heart*. I could do with them what I wanted. That's what Tyler wrote: *Do whatever you want with them—they're all yours now. U don't have to give them back.*

End of letter.

There was no order to the papers, nothing stapled or paper-clipped together, no comments or suggestions from Tyler scribbled in the margins. I started reading at random, kind of frantically, my eyes latching onto whatever word or phrase happened to jump out:

Science lab report: The frog heart has three chambers: two atria and a single ventricle. What do we humans gain by having four chambers? What are the secrets of a three-chambered heart?

Monday: memorize first two lines of Shakespeare sonnet—Betwixt mine eye and heart a league is took, And each doth good turns now unto the other—*I'll never get this right!!!!!!!!!!!!!!!!!!*

To-do list Wednesday: Write own sonnet based on Shakespeare sonnet. What rhymes with heart? *Art, bart, cart, carte, chart, dart, dartt, hardt, hart, harte, hartt, heart, mahrt, mart, marte, part, parte, schardt, smart, smartt, start, tart, tarte, tartt, apart, bossart, depart, descartes, goulart, impart, kabart, mccart, mccartt, restart.*

Alas, Descartes, you are tearing me apart at K-mart.

One of the papers was a numbered list of "heart" phrases and clichés that I read aloud: "Heartburn, eat my heart out, heart in my hand, deep in the heart of Texas, heart of the matter, heart-to-heart . . ."

I paused, asked Milo—"Why would anyone go to the trouble of making a list like that?"—didn't get an answer from him and went on reading. "The key to my heart, black heart, my heart isn't in it."

And more, plenty more, a copy of an e-valentine and a photo of a heart-shaped box of chocolates and more science class papers and more poems and drawings and pictures that were in some way heart-related. I didn't know what to make of all this. I didn't know what they added up to.

"They must mean something," I said.

"Why?"

"Why else would Tyler bother to send them?"

A yawn. Milo's voice, dreamy. "Maybe he just wants you to have them, hold on to them." Another yawn. "Keep them safe."

Safe? Safe from what?

I moved my hands through the papers like I was

clearing soap bubbles from bathwater, waiting for something hidden to surface.

And that's when it hit me—an understanding—the way that the feeling of missing a person can leap up and tug you toward it like gravity. If someone took care of these papers, if they weren't lost forever in a broken computer, if they weren't dumped in a garbage bin, they were *here.* They existed. And so in a way did Amanda. She was safe. Safe from being forgotten. Tyler needed that. And of everyone in the world, he trusted me—*me!*—to safeguard them like they were my own.

And here's the thing: The papers *were* my own. I wouldn't be giving them back. But I didn't need to feel creepy or guilty about it. Because the papers were also still Amanda's. Not part hers and part mine. All hers and all mine at the same time. I know this doesn't make sense in any logical, ordinary way. But sometimes you have to hold on to two contradictory truths. If you're going to live in the world, you have to learn to live with that.

I *could* live with that.

Milo would know what I meant, but he had dozed off. There would be plenty of time to talk about it later. His hand loosened, and the paper he was reading—the one with all the heart phrases—fluttered to the floor.

I picked it up, added it to the others, and clutched the stack of Amanda's words to my chest.

white paws, which we named Barney, short for Christiaan Barnard. That's a bit of insider transplant humor. Look it up if you need an explanation. Plus, because of my oh-so-delicate immune system, Mom splurged on an automatic, self-cleaning litter box, sale price $89.95. We saw it advertised on TV. Worth every penny.

But before all that, one of the first things I did was to clear a space on a corner of my bedroom desk. That's where I keep the stack of papers that Tyler sent to me. I placed a candle on one side of it, and a small photo of Amanda on the other. The picture came in Tyler's next letter, and I put it in a simple frame.

I don't want to give the wrong idea here. It's not like I set up a creepy religious shrine that's elevated Amanda into my personal Saint of the Holy Heart. I don't bow or pray to the picture or have sob sessions every time I look at it. I only cried the first time I put it on my desk. I lit the candle and it filled my room with a lovely scent of mango.

Honestly, there are now whole days that go by that I don't do more than glance at the picture and the papers. But I'm always aware that they're there. Safe. In my warm hands.

THIRTY-FOUR

AT FIRST TYLER'S MOM was furious that he had gone behind her back and kept all the letters from the organ recipients. After getting that reaction, he decided not to tell her how he had spied on the heart girl. But Claire eventually conceded that it was probably for the best. She was ready now. She wanted to read the letters.

They sat at the kitchen table. Tyler handed them to her one at a time. She read, passed the page to her ex-husband, read another. When she finished them all, her mouth opened; no sound came out. Her right arm reached across the table and covered Tyler's hand with her own.

In Jewish tradition, a year after a death, there's a ceremony called an unveiling. The newly erected tombstone is covered with a cloth. After prayers and words of remembrance, it's removed by the family. The Schecters decided to keep things simple. No specially engraved invitations, no big open house after the grave-side ceremony. No one wanted a repeat of the three-day madhouse of the shivah. So it would be only family and those who mattered most in their lives.

THIRTY-FIVE

THERE WAS NO ETIQUETTE book for me to turn to. Nobody ever wrote Miss Manners to ask, How do you greet the parents of your heart donor? A firm handshake? A lovely hostess gift?

And when standing by the grave, where do you keep your eyes focused? What do you do with your hands? What do you do if everyone else is crying and you're not?

What if you're the one who starts sobbing?

What if the family instantly hates you?

What do you wear?

What do you tell strangers if they ask, "And how did you know Amanda?"

What if you say the wrong thing?

What if you trip and fall facedown across the grave?

"Just because they invited us doesn't mean we have ͻ go," Mom said. "They'll understand."

But like I said, there's no etiquette book for this particular situation. How do you turn down an invitation from someone who's given you your life?

Tyler noticed them first as they walked the winding path from the parking lot to the gravesite. He couldn't read her expression and wondered if she really wanted to be there.

Thank God! It was only a small group of people. Everyone was talking and hugging, too busy to notice us. Then the brother turned. I couldn't read the expression on his face. I wondered if he really wanted me to be there.

Tyler touched his mom gently on her shoulder, gestured in their direction with his chin.

The mom looked directly at me. I didn't know what to do with my mouth. Smile? Frown? Who knew a mouth could be so much trouble? I looked down at my feet. I let Mom take my hand, even though I was too old for that. I needed to feel her. I kept walking, worried that I was kicking up too much gravel.

The two women approached each other with slow, small steps. They didn't shake hands. They didn't hug.

Claire said something to Dani's mother, who nodded once.

"She'll understand if you say no."

"I want to," I told Mom. And then Amanda's mother was standing before me. "It's okay with you?" she asked. "Just for a minute?"

Claire didn't have to stoop much. A slight bending of her knees, the wrap of her arms, a tilt of her head, and her right ear rested on Dani's chest.

It was as if all the other hugs of my life were only partial hugs, hugs where someone pulled back because they were too shy or polite or their minds were elsewhere. Or because they didn't want to feel whatever was behind the hug. It might hurt too much. It might burn. But I could feel every bit of Amanda's mom hugging every bit of me.

Tyler was thinking about how much life existed at that moment. A woman in Florida reaching out to hold her great-grandchild and a teenage boy with a new liver kissing his girlfriend and a firefighter with new lungs pulling someone from a burning building and a girl eating chocolate and a third-grader playing with her friends. And his sister in her grave, but her heart still beating and his mother listening to the steadiness of it.

My eyes met Tyler's.
I counted to eighty. Eighty beats of the heart.
Amanda's heart. My heart. Our heart.